A NEST OF NINNIES

John Ashbery & James Schuyler

A NEST OF
NINNIES

Z PRESS
CALAIS · VERMONT
1975

Chapters 1, 2, 3, 6, 9, 10, and portions of Chapters 4 and 8 first appeared in slightly different form in the following publications:

Adventures in Poetry 2, Summer 1968
Art and Literature 12, Spring 1967
Locus Solus II, Summer 1961
The Paris Review 43, Summer 1968

A NEST OF NINNIES was first published by E.P. Dutton & Co., Inc. in 1969.

Library of Congress Catalog Card Number: 75-28625
ISBN 0-915990-02-4

Cover by JOE BRAINARD

Z Press publications are edited by
KENWARD ELMSLIE

A NEST OF NINNIES

chapter one

Alice was tired. Languid, fretful, she turned to stare into her own eyes in the mirror above the mantelpiece before she spoke.

"I dislike being fifty miles from a great city. I don't know how many cars pass every day and it makes me wonder."

Marshall smiled at her and continued to remove the plastic covers from a number of dishes he had just extracted from the icebox. Kicking out her housecoat, Alice moved to the kitchen table and picked up a chicken wing.

"I don't know what you're keeping in that icebox, but it makes everything taste funny."

"It must be that half a cantaloupe you didn't eat," Marshall said agreeably, "though I don't see how with these covers."

"I don't know what you're trying to prove. I don't think you will either. Unless you're trying to imply that I don't eat because I'm unhappy, which I readily admit."

"Now, Alice, please don't put those wing bones back in the bowl."

"Why don't you admit that you enjoy my unhappiness?"

"A supper of leftovers isn't a very cheerful prospect, but that's the price of entertaining guests. I could have made a casserole out of these things, but you always say you like to know what you're eating. You didn't seem so unhappy last night."

"What happened last night? You certainly can't mean that a pickup supper and a rummy game would affect my spirits."

Marshall made no reply, but dumped some cole slaw into a dish that already had pickled beets in it. Alice went to the window and looked out of it, as though commenting on the view which it disclosed. On the six-lane superhighway just beyond the hedge, cars thundered by, bound for dramatic New York.

"If you'll set the table," Marshall said, "it will be all ready to eat."

Alice turned from the window in a dazed way and began dreamily to lay out the California dinnerware.

"Seriously, I prefer to eat in the dining room," Marshall said. "It's nicer."

"Look, Fifi," Alice said, "let's stop kidding ourselves. I want to go to the city."

"Where's the basket for the bread? It's hot."

"Marshall, I want to go to the city."

"There's nothing to do in the city at night. Besides, I have to go there every day," he added in a sulky tone.

"Now you're cross perhaps you'll tell me the truth: aren't you unhappy?"

"No, and I don't think it's too good an idea to spend time in thinking about things like that."

"How else do you suggest I spend my time—eating?"

"Dear, I can see you're not yourself, so if you'd like to go to a movie, fine. I wouldn't even be averse to going into the city, provided of course we don't take the car."

Alice threw some food onto her plate and wouldn't answer.

"The bread will be too dry to eat if we don't find that basket soon."

"Who knows, maybe I threw it out with the leftover Korn Kurls."

This seemed to wound Marshall. Then he discovered the bread basket propping up a copy of Life on the back of the range. It was open to a two-page photograph of the New York skyline. Marshall served the bread, and for some minutes an ill-natured silence reigned. Soon both realized that the house had begun to grow quite cold.

"I suppose I forgot to shake the furnace again," Alice said. But neither stirred. "I suppose I should go shake it or look at it." She pushed away the bowl of beets and slaw which Marshall had not offered her. "I suppose if I did want to go to the movies, you'd try to get me to go to one in town."

"You seem to think I am patience itself," Marshall said. Suddenly there came a gentle tapping at the kitchen door. Alice got up from the table and went down into the basement. Marshall glided across the room with careful steps to admit their visitor. It was a small, very pretty young woman.

"You are probably eating," she said, "and wonder why I came to the side door."

"We usually eat in the dining room," Marshall said, gazing beyond her at a few flakes of snow which had begun to fall. "Snow always makes me think of my childhood," he muttered

11

as he shut the door after she had passed into the unlighted kitchen.

"Someone seems to be trying to break your furnace," murmured the now almost invisible girl. "I came over because the radio says it's going to snow. There weren't any lights in front."

"Wouldn't you like to sit down and eat something?" Marshall asked, stifling a yawn. "We're eating in the kitchen to economize on heating bills. Alice likes to feel there's something going into the bank."

The guest pulled her fur coat more tightly about her shoulders and looked about the room with apparent interest. "I think a fireplace in your kitchen is lovely. It makes a very nice room of it."

"We of course made no attempt to alter this old place when we took it over, beyond a few slight repairs." Marshall seemed aware of the young woman for the first time. "I wanted to have the fireplace bricked up because it cools the house, but so many people commented on it we decided to leave it."

"You don't seem to see so many people."

"Look, snow is coming down it now."

An especially loud clang from the basement caused them both to start. "You sit down and I'll get you a cup of coffee. I'll put on the lights and call Alice," Marshall announced.

Alice's dim form appeared in the door. "I think I've just blown a fuse. Hello, Fabia."

"That's very funny. The fuses at our house blew out too. It must be general."

"We have no more fuses," Marshall said. "I should hate to go anywhere and come back to a dark house."

"Fat chance," Alice said. "Why, it's snowing." She went to the kitchen door and opened it.

"We could watch television in the dark," Marshall said to Fabia. "Except of course the set wouldn't work either. But we might light some candles and play rummy after I wash the dishes, if Alice is through eating."

Alice had taken a few steps outside into the yard. A chill wind made the kitchen unbearable. Fabia and Marshall drew closer together. "I'm not sure I'm equal to rummy two nights in a row," Fabia said. "But you better hunt up the candles before it's too dark to find them."

"My dears, I can't tell you how divinely bracing it is out," Alice said returning. "We simply must take a walk, at least as far as the shopping center."

"We could buy some fuses," Marshall said.

Their departure was complicated by Marshall's discovery that the electricity was still on in half of the house. "All the television in the world won't make the rest of the lights work," Alice said. "If you're coming with us, take off that apron."

"It's too bad you didn't take your coat off in the house, Fabia," Marshall said as they walked down the drive. "I'm afraid you'll catch cold now."

"I never catch cold," Fabia said.

Alice persisted in her mood of spiritual exaltation. "Look at the trees and telephone wires," she said. "On a night like this New York doesn't compel me so much."

"You always talk of New York as though it were a thousand miles away," Fabia said. "You know you can go there any time you want to." Alice and Marshall ignored this remark.

The snow was fine and dry, the temperature slightly below freezing. They walked past a deserted skating rink, and a group of fir trees which the Rotary Club had caused to be hung with lights. Further on, where the superhighway became a cloverleaf, they turned off to the right, and bought some fuses at a hardware store which had officially closed. Fabia suggested they have a drink at a nearby Howard Johnson's.

"You two go ahead if you like," Alice said. "I'll walk around in the snow and wait for you."

"I don't know as we ought to have left her alone," Marshall said as they entered the dining room. "When Alice is feeling inspired, she often goes to unusual lengths to prevent herself from looking silly."

"What could she do on her own?" Fabia asked.

"I think this is quite a pleasant place," Marshall said. "If Alice gets tired she will probably go home. She has the fuses."

Fabia paid her customary respects to the new surroundings, and then lapsed into the sorrowful silence which was her natural state.

In one corner a big jukebox whose revolving lights cast an ominous glow on the ceiling was playing "Dance to My Lady." The walls featured pagan scenes. Beside the cash register stood an opaque glass vase of imitation snapdragons. Marshall ordered their drinks from the brisk and frilly waitress in a way that showed they were not on a date. He ordered a straight whiskey and Fabia a cuba libre.

Fabia said, "You seem so little aware of me when I am with you, Marshall, I wonder if you ever think of me when I'm not. I know I often muse about you and Alice and your little house."

"It always amazes me we are near neighbors," Marshall replied. "Alice and I tend to be people who lead somewhat isolated lives because they are self-sufficient."

Fabia said, "I too lead an isolated life but not for that reason."

Marshall looked shifty. "I hope you won't confide in me," he said.

"I think you really like it though you say you don't. Anyway there's very little to confide in anyone about my humdrum existence. I'm not one of your mystery divorcées or widows."

14

"That sounds like a confidence to me," Marshall replied glumly.

"When I was young," Fabia hinted, "I told many unmotivated lies. Once I told my mother my baby brother had fallen down and seriously injured himself. This upset my mother, not because I was lying, but because she was superstitious and thought it might come true. A few days later my brother came down with scarlet fever."

"I wonder what's become of Alice," Marshall said, "unless she has gone home or is still walking around."

"Another time I told Daddy there was a fire in the chimney. Nobody would believe me and the house nearly burned down."

"That's funny. I used to be afraid the house would catch fire and we would have to go out into the snow at night, like poor people."

"I don't think that's interesting," Fabia said. Marshall looked hurt. "I bet you think about your childish fears a great deal," she went on spitefully.

"Of all the sneaky tricks," Marshall exploded. "I wish Alice were here to see this."

"Don't be such an old bozo," Fabia said. "Don't you know when you're being teased?"

"That is precisely what I was objecting to. We ought to go immediately, but I think I need another drink against the weather."

"Me too," Fabia said. "It looks like a veritable blizzard outside."

Alice came in. There was a lot of snow on her hair and on her coat. "It really is a blizzard," she said. "You won't be able to go to the city tomorrow, Marshall."

"What makes you think the trains won't run?" Marshall asked.

"We might as well order another round while we're waiting," Fabia said quickly.

"You and Marshall are just alike," Alice said.

The waitress took the order but had not yet brought the drinks when Dr. and Mrs. Bridgewater appeared in the dining room. "Perhaps you could settle the bill, Marshall," Fabia murmured, "on the side when we go."

"I thought you had your money," Marshall growled. "I certainly didn't bring any."

"Oh shush," Alice said. "Good evening, Dr. and Mrs. Bridgewater. Isn't it freshening out? Isn't it a nice night?"

"Why yes it is," said Dr. Bridgewater with a smile that grew broader, "yes it is."

"On our way here we passed at least six cars that had gone into the ditch," Mrs. Bridgewater said. "Good evening, one and all."

"Here are your *eau de vies*," said the waitress. "Did you two wish to order?"

"What pleasant-looking drinks," Mrs. Bridgewater said. "Are they alcoholic?"

"They are among the strongest drinks known to man," Dr. Bridgewater commented in a placid manner. "No, young lady, we do not wish to order anything. Unless you would like something, Mother. I think I will have one of your coffee sodas."

"Is it too late to get something to eat?" Mrs. Bridgewater asked. "I would like some filet of sole. I'm only joking. I'll have a coffee soda too. No, I'll have a pineapple."

"I could fix you a nice steak sandwich," the waitress said.

"Just the sodas," Dr. Bridgewater said. "She wouldn't want anything solid on her stomach this time of night."

"I think I'd like just a taste of yours, Fabia dear," Mrs. Bridgewater said. Fabia silently passed her the small glass. Mrs.

Bridgewater took a healthy swallow of the powerful liqueur without visible effect.

"Fabia's mother and I had a terrible shock today," Dr. Bridgewater explained. "We learned that Fabia's brother has flunked out of college." Fabia seemed annoyed at their mentioning it.

Alice giggled. "I can't wait to hear Victor's version," she said.

"We have just heard it," Dr. Bridgewater sighed. "Victor arrived home from Syracuse this evening. He is outside in the car. He said he would rather not come in."

Alice looked coldly at Fabia. "I'm dying to see Victor," she said. "Do let's all finish up here. I think I'll go ask him if he wouldn't like to walk me home on this beautiful snowy evening."

"Of course neither Alice nor I has any intention of walking on a night like this," Marshall said before Dr. Bridgewater could reply. "We should very much appreciate your driving us home. I shall have to be up at the crack of dawn to learn if any trains will run."

"I'm glad Victor's back," Fabia said. "There is no pretense between us."

"Yes, I'm glad to have my boy at home," Mrs. Bridgewater said.

"Are we going to sit here all night?" Alice said. "It's no part of my plans."

They paid the check and went out into the snowstorm. Near the Bridgewaters' car a boy of about eighteen was building a snowman. "That's a nice one," Alice said, "it looks like Howard Johnson himself."

"Hi, Alice," Victor said seriously. "I would have made it bigger but the snow is too dry."

"I know," Alice said.

"Is that what they taught you to do in college?" Fabia asked.

"I don't want to have to speak to you again, Fabia," Dr. Bridgewater said. "Now if we will all arrange ourselves in the car, I think we can trust Victor to drive us home safely."

"Put not thy trust in things of this world," Fabia chuckled.

Mrs. Bridgewater slipped into the seat next to her son ahead of Alice. "I thought you'd never come out of there," Victor said. "I started to build a snowman to keep my circulation going."

"Look how fast the snow is falling in the headlights," Alice said over the thudding of the chains. "Much faster than when you're walking in it." Mrs. Bridgewater began to hum a Presbyterian theme, and Marshall joined in with the words in a muted baritone.

"Oh those crazy fraternity boys," Victor said apropos of nothing.

"Victor, Elm Avenue is one way," Dr. Bridgewater said after a while.

"I thought this was Spruce Avenue," Victor said.

"It happens to be Seminole Path," Marshall said. "I couldn't imagine where you were going."

Victor turned off the street into a likely looking driveway where the car promptly stuck in a drift, nor could their best efforts dislodge it.

chapter two

"What are you going to do today, Fabia?" Victor asked.

"I'm well into *The Sweet Cheat Gone*," Fabia said, "but I may put it aside. I don't want ever to finish Proust. I might just go into New York. I read of a big sale of modern painting reproductions in yesterday's *Times*. I wonder if Marshall is having lunch with anyone."

"How do you know he went to work?" Victor said, getting up from the table.

"I didn't say he had," Fabia said lightly.

"No one could accuse my children," Dr. Bridgewater said in a tone much like his daughter's, "of stealing the bread out of the mouths of hardworking people."

"I certainly hope you're not going to get any more pictures," Martha said, from the pantry. "We have enough of them around here."

"I don't know why you say that, Dad," Mrs. Bridgewater said. "You know you wouldn't want Fabia living in the city away from home. And I certainly wouldn't want her to have the exhaustion of commuting."

"But I get tired of just sitting around the house all day," Fabia said. "I wonder if I could get a job in Marshall's office."

"Why don't you quit beating around the bush and propose to him?" Victor said, winking at his mother.

"Perhaps because I'm afraid it might occur to Alice to propose to you," Fabia said tartly.

"If you are going into New York," Dr. Bridgewater said, "I wish you'd go past the tobacconist's and find out why I have not received my cigars."

Marshall looked askance at an office boy who laid some papers on his desk. "Those should go in my 'in' tray, not on my desk," he said. "You must be new here."

"Yes, sir," the boy said, leaving the office.

"Did the snow cause much trouble out your way?" Miss Burgoyne asked. Miss Burgoyne (Betty to the other secretaries in the firm) was older than Marshall and this showed in her manner toward him.

"Yes. Did it where you live?"

"No it hardly snowed at all where we are," Miss Burgoyne replied, "but I don't know how I would have known because I didn't poke my head out of doors the entire weekend."

"Playing Chinese checkers?" Marshall said with a sneer.

"That boy brought you the wrong papers," Miss Burgoyne pointed out. "These are clearly marked 'Claims.' "

"It doesn't matter. I wanted to dictate some letters right now anyway."

"Perhaps they need these papers up in Claims," Miss Burgoyne said patiently.

"That's not my lookout. Buzz the mail room for a messenger." Miss Burgoyne picked up Marshall's ringing phone and reported, "There's a Miss Bridgewater to see you. Shall I say you're busy?"

"I wonder if something's wrong at home. Have her come in, and since you're not busy, would you mind running these papers upstairs yourself?"

"Mr. Bush can see Miss Bridgewater now," Miss Burgoyne said smoothly. She took the offending papers and left.

"I hope I didn't drag you out of a conference or anything," Fabia said. "I envy you businessmen your snug little offices."

"Is there something wrong at home?" Marshall asked.

"I don't know," Fabia said absently, "I haven't talked to Alice today. But I imagine you would have heard from Victor if there were," she added, taking the chair Miss Burgoyne had recently vacated. "Was that the secretary you say is so bossy? I'm going shopping later for some reproductions of modern paintings. Perhaps I could give you a couple to brighten up your walls. I was wondering if you might care to have lunch at some fairly inexpensive place since I don't get my allowance till day after tomorrow. Say, do you think I could get a job here?"

"Certainly, if you can do typing and shorthand," Marshall said. "I was going to have my lunch sent up."

"Oh come on, you're not all that busy." Fabia had commenced hooking some paper clips together so they formed a chain.

"Did your father send you here to spy on me?"

"Actually, I type faster than some touch typists. Aren't there any positions that don't call for shorthand?"

"Only in the shipping department," Marshall said good-humoredly.

"Don't you have any call for receptionists or girl messengers or some kind of job that requires a uniform so I wouldn't have to keep my mind on my work?"

"I suppose I could ask Mr. Kelso," Marshall said.

"Oh well, I wouldn't want to start for about a month," Fabia said with a sudden lack of interest. "Why don't we go have some grub?"

Miss Burgoyne came in all out of breath. "If you're trying to offend me by imitating Alice," Marshall was saying, "you are."

"Excuse me, Mr. Bush," Miss Burgoyne said, "but I was wondering whether you want to dictate these letters right away. My mother and father have come into town to have lunch with me and they want very much to meet you."

"But I did meet them last year at the office party."

"I know, but they've forgotten what you're like."

"You could have met them and had it over with by now," Fabia said. "I mean, it's lunchtime and we're all hungry."

"Oh here they are," Miss Burgoyne said, with a glance over her shoulder. "Shall I tell them to go away?"

"Hello there, Mr. Bush," Mrs. Burgoyne said, ducking her head a little.

Fabia stood up, smiling graciously, as though in the presence of the Burgoynes her fur coat took on an added luster. "Why don't we all have lunch together?" she said. "I am Fabia Bridgewater."

"These are my parents," Miss Burgoyne said to Marshall.

"Yes," Marshall said, "I remember meeting them very well. Let's eat." He pushed back the chair from which he had risen and took his topcoat off a hanger behind the door.

Mr. Kelso, a portly man in a brown overcoat and hat, and matching yellow wool scarf and gloves, materialized. "Oh dear," he said, "I hope you haven't forgotten our lunch date, Marshall."

"I'm afraid he's had a visitation," Fabia said. "This is Mr. and Mrs. Burgoyne, Miss Burgoyne's parents. I am Fabia Bridgewater. Marshall and I are neighbors."

"I'm Irving Kelso," Mr. Kelso said. "May I ask permission to crash the party?"

"I suppose this confirms all your notions about the amount of loafing that gets done in offices," Marshall said to Mr. Burgoyne, who shrugged.

"Whose handiwork is this?" Mr. Kelso asked, picking up the chain of paper clips and shaking it lightly so it danced back and forth.

"Mine," Fabia said. "When I was at school we used to wear them like that with our sweaters. Instead of the conventional pearls."

"I like your fur coat," Miss Burgoyne said to Fabia in the elevator. "I was going to get a fur one last year, but somehow they look awful on me."

"I like yours," Fabia said, "but I hate fur-trimmed coats. I think people should either get a fur coat or a plain cloth coat."

"Shall it be Childs?" Mr. Kelso asked as they passed the building directory, which was framed in brass oak leaves. "I must say, this certainly makes a pleasant change from our cut-and-dried routine."

"This is such a swank building, Mr. Kelso," Fabia said, "I suppose you only hire Sarah Lawrence girls who know typing and shorthand."

"Ha-ha," Mr. Kelso said. "But if you're serious you can always drop in on our Personnel Department any morning before ten and tell them about yourself. There's always room in the firm for a pleasing personality."

"In the lower salary brackets, at any rate," Marshall said.

"I make it a rule never to cross against the light," Mrs. Burgoyne said, stopping short at the curb.

23

"I'm afraid you'll get us all arrested, Mother," Miss Burgoyne said, mystifyingly.

"The perils of the machine age," Fabia said. Despite these, however, the party was soon comfortably seated at one of the larger tables in Childs.

"Why don't we all have the oysters Rockefeller?" Marshall said.

"I don't see those on my menu," Mrs. Burgoyne said.

"Mr. Bush was joking," Miss Burgoyne said. "The menu has the cheese fondue on toast tips I told you about," she added. "But I don't know if you'd like it."

"Do you get into town much?" Mr. Kelso asked Mrs. Burgoyne pleasantly.

"Let's give our orders, Irving, then talk," Fabia said. They did so, though the ordering took some little time.

"I don't see why they always serve you a double order of toast when you order things on toast points," Mrs. Burgoyne said.

"I am ready to fall to with a hearty goodwill," Mr. Kelso said, beginning to eat.

"I think part of that toast was intended for me," Fabia said sweetly.

"Betty, you better ask the waitress to bring her a plate to put her toast on," Mrs. Burgoyne said.

"Excuse the mistake," the waitress said, removing the toast; "I'll bring you some bread."

"Would you mind bringing me a knife or something to stir my coffee with?" Marshall asked, to the amusement of all.

"I always wonder what men talk about at their lunches," Miss Burgoyne said archly. The cheese fondue seemingly had affected her like wine. "I suppose they talk about business," she went on, "but that isn't what they look like they're talking about." She lapsed into sudden silence.

"By the way, did those papers ever get to Claims?" Marshall asked.

"No," Miss Burgoyne said with a giggle, "I tore them into little pieces and dropped them down the mail chute."

Mrs. Burgoyne began to laugh and kept it up for quite a time. When she regained control of herself, she said, "Betty, you'll be the death of me."

"Are you a commuter like the rest of us, Irving?" Fabia asked casually.

"I'm afraid I'm that rare bird, a born New Yorker," Mr. Kelso said. "Personally, I'd like to try the suburbs, but it wouldn't suit Mother. You see, I live with my mother and she's getting on."

"Isn't that funny, I live with my mother too," Fabia said.

"And your father, and your brother," Marshall said.

"Do you have any brothers or sisters, Miss Burgoyne?" Fabia asked.

"Yes, we have a son who has an auto-supply store in Teaneck," Mrs. Burgoyne said. "He owns his own building and he and my daughter-in-law and three grandchildren live over the store."

"Mr. Bush has seen their pictures," Miss Burgoyne said. "And I have seen some pictures of his charming home. You were in one of them" she added, speaking directly to Fabia. "I think it was at a New Year's Eve party or something. At any rate you were in one of those strapless gowns."

Mrs. Burgoyne looked at Fabia as though identifying someone of whom she had heard.

"Ever done any curling?" Mr. Burgoyne said to Irving Kelso.

"Yes." Mr. Kelso allowed a pause to become pregnant, and then went on. "While I was overseas in the Air Corps, I went for a rest leave to a castle turned over to the Army in Scotland. By the time I left, I was curling like a native."

"Did you ever run into a Scotch mist?" Mr. Burgoyne inquired.

"No," Mr. Kelso said, "but there was a ghost in the castle where I stayed. It appeared to everyone on their birthdays, and as luck would have it, my birthday occurred during my stay there. About one o'clock in the morning of my birthday, the door of my room opened and a figure clad in white came slowly toward me. I felt sure it was the ghost, but it was only the nurse come to give me a little scare and ask me if there was anything I needed. I told her, excuse the expression, to get the hell out."

"Then you were the only one who didn't really see the ghost?" Miss Burgoyne asked.

"I was coming to that," Mr. Kelso said. "About eleven o'clock in the evening of my birthday, another white-clad figure entered my room: the ghost. It passed close to me and murmured my name, Irving, in tones that I remember to this day."

"Are you Roman Catholic?" Mr. Burgoyne asked.

" 'Irving' sounds like an odd name for a ghost to murmur," Marshall said.

"No, Presbyterian," Mr. Kelso said.

"It's not half as funny as if it murmured 'Marshall,' " Fabia said.

"Did it murmur the name of each person in the castle on their birthday?" Miss Burgoyne asked.

"I don't know about that," Mr. Kelso said, "but I know that on one other occasion, when a fellow from Wisconsin had a birthday, all the candles on the cake were blown out by an unseen force."

"It's a good thing we're hearing these creepy stories in a brightly lit restaurant at noon," Mrs. Burgoyne said.

"Usually people don't believe me when I tell them about it,"

Mr. Kelso said. "In fact, without the testimony of my own senses, I wouldn't believe it either."

"I don't think I've ever thought about ghosts," Fabia said. "I suppose there isn't any reason not to believe in them, especially if you've seen one. There's a house at the end of our block that's supposed to be haunted."

"I never heard that about any house in your block," Marshall said. "I think you're giving your imagination free rein."

"What sort of ghosts is it supposed to have?" Mr. Kelso asked.

"It's not supposed to have ghosts so much as noises and cries," Fabia said.

"That could be said of almost any house in your block," Marshall said.

"What kind of a neighborhood are these people going to imagine I live in, Marshall? It's a lot quieter than living on a six-lane highway."

"Perhaps some boys got into the house and made the noises," Mrs. Burgoyne suggested. This remark cause the other members of the luncheon party to become aware of the hour.

"Are we going to have time for dessert?" Miss Burgoyne asked.

"We're a great family for desserts," Mrs. Burgoyne said. "You ought to hear these two wrangling over the last piece of fudge layer."

"I never eat them," Fabia said, "but if you're going to have one, I think I'll have a liqueur. Do you have any crème de café?" she asked the waitress.

"Sure," the waitress said. "Any more liqueurs?"

"We can't let a lady drink alone, can we, Marshall?" Mr. Kelso said.

"Sometimes it's difficult to stop them," Marshall said.

"That sounds like a heavenly idea," Mrs. Burgoyne said. "Would you like a B & B, Father?" The order resolved itself into four B & B's, one crème de café and a Drambuie for Mr. Kelso.

"What is that tune coming over the Muzak?" Mrs. Burgoyne asked.

"The 'Intermezzo' from *The Jewels of the Madonna,* surely?" Mr. Kelso said.

"Doesn't Alice play this on her cello?" Fabia asked Marshall.

"I didn't know your sister was musical." Miss Burgoyne sounded hurt. "I'm intensely musical, though I don't read a note."

"Alice is musical," Fabia explained, "and I read a great deal."

"I try to read what's on the best-seller list," Mr. Kelso said, "but sometimes I can't stand the smut that gets printed."

"Separate checks?" the waitress asked.

"Some people just don't like to act as if they think the other person is right too soon," Alice said to Victor. "For instance, he still won't admit that he's gotten to like instant coffee. I don't mean that it's as good as the other kind, but you do get to like it."

"Why don't you blindfold him sometime and make him taste both to see if he can tell the difference?" Victor said.

Alice looked vaguely at her cello case and didn't answer. The water on the stove came to a boil. Victor got up and fetched it. "Sometimes his nagging is enough to turn my stomach," he suggested.

"Leave a little room for the cream," Alice said. "It tastes vile without it."

"At Syracuse my roommate made me think of Marshall all the time. No matter what I was doing, it seemed I should be doing something else. If I was studying I should have been at a football rally. And of course if I went to the movies I should have been studying. Once he went so far as to lock me in my room to prevent my attending a football rally. But I got even."

"What did you do?" Alice asked languidly.

"I put snow in his shoes. Just before he put them on. So it wouldn't melt and ruin them."

"What time are you going to pick me up after my cello lesson?"

"What time will you be through?"

"I'll tell you when we get there," Alice said. "Last night when I was walking in the snow I thought I would spend all of today out in it. I've scarcely stirred out of the house except to walk Marshall to the station and come home by a roundabout way."

"I like the out-of-doors, but not that much. What do you think about when you're outside all day?"

Alice smiled. "It's funny you should say that, because I do think differently out of doors. In the house I think about how much I want to get to New York, and when I'm outside I think about how it will be when I do get there. You know, the way I'll fix the apartment and evenings at concerts."

"You seem like too much of a nature-lover to be settling down in a skyscraper," Victor said.

"You can't have everything," Alice said. "What are your plans for the future?"

Victor answered seriously and decisively. "My family can't get it through their heads that even though I flunked out of school I won't be a professional man of some sort. When I get them straightened out I want to get a job on a boat and see something of the world."

"Let's get out of here," Alice said. "That nutty cello teacher starts charging me for his time on the stroke of the hour."

Luckily they arrived at Professor Scott's at the appointed time. Professor Scott was just opening the front door to look for her. "Leave galoshes on the porch," he cautioned. "Is Victor coming in to wait?"

"No, he isn't," Alice said. "Come back in an hour if you want to walk me home, Victor."

"You can come back here and wait if you get too cold," the professor said kindly. "I'm used to having young people around."

The room in which the cello lessons were given was filled with wicker furniture, ferns and stuffed birds under glass. It was so cold that frost congealed on the windowpanes, making it difficult for pupils to see the music as well as to perform it.

The telephone rang in the hall. "Now who can that be?" the professor said, leaving the room. He returned shortly. "Did you make an arrangement to exchange times with Abel Greeley when you were here last?" he asked. "At any rate, his mother seems to think so, and she's on her way here with him now. It seems he has some terribly important engagement later this afternoon."

"That's great," Alice said. "What am I supposed to do meanwhile in this freezing place?"

"I know it's a terrible imposition," Professor Scott said cringingly, "but Abel's mother is so important in the P.T.A. that I'm afraid my practice will suffer if I seem to offend her. You could stick around during his lesson and try your hand at the violin; we could play some trios. I wouldn't charge you for it."

"Oh all right, but you can't blame me for feeling peeved," Alice said.

"I'm sorry to take away your lesson time, Alice," Abel said. "Mother wants me to go to some party with her. She thinks her women friends are going to find a twelve-year-old trundling around with a cello a remarkable sight."

"I'm terribly mortified, Alice," Mrs. Greeley said. "Abel seemed to think he had exchanged times with you at his last lesson."

"Next time why don't we communicate by telephone?"

Alice said. "What a becoming hat, Mrs. Greeley. Navy goes very nicely with those colors."

"I'm afraid it's a little impractical for this blustery day," Mrs. Greeley said, eyeing Alice's attire.

"We had best set to work," Professor Scott laughed. "Mrs. Greeley, would you care to be Deems Taylor during this performance, or would you rather wait in the other room?"

"Mmm, perhaps I'll do that," Mrs. Greeley said. "I saw Victor Bridgewater there on my way in and I've been wanting to have a chat with him."

"Oh, hello, ma'am," Victor said, looking up from a copy of *Liberty*. "I saw you come in just now."

"I've been meaning to have a chat with you, Victor," Mrs. Greeley said. "How does it happen you're home in midterm?"

"I'm not going to college anymore," Victor said. "Are you going to sit down and wait too?"

Mrs. Greeley settled herself on a settee covered in slippery horsehair. "Isn't this a rather sudden decision?" she asked. "It must be very upsetting for your mother. Children can be so thoughtless." She smiled gently at Victor.

"It wasn't my decision," Victor said. He laughed rather loudly.

"My, somebody seems to be very badly out of key in there," Mrs. Greeley said after a thoughtful pause. "Are you planning to take up the study of music, Victor?"

"No," Victor said. "From what I hear I guess Abel has a pretty big future ahead of him in that line."

"I suppose so," Mrs. Greeley said, "but on the other hand," she continued with a sudden burst of frankness, "though he is talented in many areas, he never seems to take an interest in anything."

"That's the way I used to be," Victor said.

"No, Abel, not in triplets," Professor Scott was saying. "What's the sense in my marking things in your music if you don't play them? Alice was right that time, you've got to admit."

"OK, Casals," Abel said, "let's hear you take it."

"I'm certainly glad I never took up the violin," Alice said. "It's so confusing not having something to lean on."

Professor Scott sighed and shook his head. "This trio was certainly a mistake. One of you is impudent and the other silly. Excuse me, Miss Bush, but it's the only word that suits." He handed them their parts for a piece of music described on its cover as, "Exercise for Two Stringed Instruments and Piano."

"Are you sure you want us to go through with this?" Abel asked.

"Sarcasm is a dangerous habit to cultivate, Abel. It may color your whole life and make your future bitter," Professor Scott said serenely.

"Oh come on," Alice growled, "let's finish this up before I catch pneumonia."

"You don't look like an incipient victim of pneumonia," Professor Scott said.

"I see sarcasm has not left your life uncolored," Abel said.

Professor Scott turned to gaze out the window at the somber landscape. Mrs. Greeley appeared, smiling, in the door. "You look like a study of the young Mozart and family. But I fear I must whisk Abel off."

"Don't apologize, Mrs. Greeley," Professor Scott said. "No, that's all right; I couldn't take any money for this lesson."

"Oh, Abel," Mrs. Greeley said, looking at her son with secret pride.

"I don't suppose for a change you would like to carry the cello," Abel said.

"No, I would not," Mrs. Greeley laughed. "Now hop to it, you little imp."

Victor and Alice, in order to enjoy the effect of the sunset upon the snow, walked home by way of the park. The park was a square area planted with elm trees. In the center of it there was a statue of a Confederate soldier, presented to the town by a town of the same name in a Southern state, where, presumably, a statue of a Union soldier was to be found.

chapter three

"Miss Alice Bush," Irving Kelso said, "her brother and my co-worker, Mr. Marshall Bush, and—excuse me, Fabia—Miss Fabia Bridgewater, their neighbor and friend. My mother, Mrs. Kelso."

"How do you do," Mrs. Kelso said. "This is Fluffy. He's a little out of sorts today, so don't pay too much attention to him."

No one made any motion toward the white cat which lay, outstretched and watchful, at Mrs. Kelso's feet. Fluffy got up and left the room. "Oh dear," Mrs. Kelso said, "it must be one of you doesn't like cats."

"Would you country people like a drink before dinner?"

Irving said. "We have gin, rum, bourbon, rye, rock and rye, Swedish punch and crème de menthe."

"I'm sure they would all like to sit down first, Irving," Mrs. Kelso said. "Won't you please seat yourselves?"

Fabia and Irving sat down on a tiny love seat, and Marshall on an antique wooden chair. Alice sat on the piano bench. "This looks like one of those chairs guests aren't supposed to sit on," Marshall said.

"No, it's extremely sturdy," Mrs. Kelso said.

Irving took a white handkerchief out of the breast pocket of his jacket and held it across his forehead. "Your orders for drinks?" he said in a falsetto voice.

Everyone decided to try the Swedish punch except Mrs. Kelso, who poured herself a small glass of an unidentified liquid. The Swedish punch was served in tall, ruby-colored goblets with clear stems.

"What a lovely painting, Mrs. Kelso," Fabia said. "Did some member of your family do it?"

"Yes, they did," Mrs. Kelso said, "and no one so very far away."

"Could that be the famous haunted castle?" Fabia asked.

"It has certain features of that castle," Irving said with a blush, "but the basic idea came from my own head."

"I heard a most interesting broadcast today," Mrs. Kelso said firmly. Fluffy entered the room carrying a dead mouse.

"Funny, I never noticed that place on the ceiling before," Irving said.

"If you're looking at the place I am," Fabia said, "I think it's the shadow of the knob on that lamp."

"You look terribly uncomfortable, Mr. Bush," Mrs. Kelso said. "Why don't you sit on one of the less ornamental chairs. In the broadcast I heard," she went on, "a scientist explained how very close our planet is to being drained of its natural resources. He seemed to think it quite likely we would run out of them before men have learned how to harness solar energy or the tides, in which case we would all either starve or freeze."

"Oh, Mildred," Irving said, "he sounds like that discredited alarmist to me."

"I'm sure it made very good sense as he explained it," Mrs. Kelso said. "The first thing to go will be coal."

"We could all go down South and live, until the food started running low," Alice suggested pleasantly.

"Collard greens with salt pork? Not for me thank you," Fabia said.

"I don't think it's a joking matter," Mrs. Kelso said.

"Are these goblets Bohemian glass?" Marshall asked.

"Of course I don't know why I'm critizing you," Mrs. Kelso said, ignoring Marshall. "Being an inveterate apartment dweller, I'd be totally hamstrung if the electricity or the gas were to go off."

"By the by, Marshall," Fabia said, "I bought those reproductions of modern paintings. You must choose some for your office, if you'd like to have some."

"A funny thing happened at the office today," Irving said. "There's a new girl in accounts receivable . . ."

A maid silently entered the room and withdrew to indicate dinner was served. To reach the dining room it was necessary for the guests to file down a long hall past several shut doors. The hall was hung with etchings of various New York skyscrapers under construction.

"I thought you said there were no positions open in your office, Marshall," Fabia said.

"I'm not in personnel," Marshall said.

"I love these pictures of New York, always in a state of becoming," Alice said.

"Though high buildings going up must have been more exciting when there weren't so many," somebody else said.

The guests took their places at the table. The dinner menu was as follows: salted nuts in small dishes, a relish of olives and celery stuffed with Roquefort cheese spread, consommè madriléne, broiled lamb chops, green peas and new potatoes, tomato aspic salad, baked Alaska. Rolls and demitasse. The demitasse was served in the living room.

"Tell me more about this new girl in the office, Irving," Fabia said. "I hope she's a shorthand champion so that I won't be forced to take issue with Marshall over his not having told me about the opening."

"That reminds me of what I was going to tell you. You see, Miss Markle—her name—is a speed typist. This afternoon the electric speedwriter she uses went haywire. She was typing some multiforms and they came out of the roller all scorched."

"Marshall's secretary doesn't sound very bright on the phone," Alice said. "You could probably replace her, Fabia, if you're set on becoming a useful member of society."

"Marshall would be too much the slave driver," Fabia said. "Besides, I couldn't go gunning for the job of someone I've met."

"Miss Burgoyne is invaluable," Irving said.

"Not if she keeps hinting around after a raise, she isn't," Marshall said.

"I'm sorry I can't invite you to watch television," Mrs. Kelso said. "Irving refuses to have a set in the house."

"Oh, Mother," Irving said, "it isn't as though you cared for it yourself. You know what you say about how the antennas look on all the roofs whenever we go out driving. What's that you're humming, Alice?"

"It's from Haydn's *Surprise Symphony*," Alice said. "Say, would you mind if I browsed through your record collection?"

"As though you could stop her," Fabia murmured.

Alice pulled out a modern sonata for unaccompanied cello and slipped it dexterously onto the turntable.

"You see," Mrs. Kelso said as the first notes filled the room, "I told you some guest would enjoy playing it sometime."

Alice turned down the volume. "I wondered how it got in with all that bagpipe music."

"Those were the gift of Scottish friends," Irving said, "who had once owned the castle where I spent my rest leave. They were awfully nice to us fellows. They even tried to get me to eat some haggis, the national dish of Scotland."

Marshall, who was sitting in a Cogswell chair, gave a start. "I see I'm having my usual after-dinner effect on you," Fabia said lightly. "Perhaps we should put on something livelier before he drifts off altogether," she explained to the other guests. "What is that record with the bright-colored cover I can see from here?"

"A few of F.D.R.'s more cogent speeches," Mrs. Kelso said. "No, thank you," she said to the maid, who was passing a silver bowl filled with lumps of sugar. She turned to the others. "They think I'm funny," she said, "but I never take sugar in my coffee after a sweet dessert."

"Maybe this will be more to Fabia's liking," Alice said, taking off the cello sonata and putting on a doleful Highland lament.

"Good grief," Marshall said.

"What happened to that record of opera encores you bought, Sonny?" Mrs. Kelso asked.

"Music hath charms," Irving said, "but a rousing game of Monopoly might be more to the point."

"Do you all like to look at colored slides?" Mrs. Kelso asked. "Irving has some perfectly beautiful views of Florida and northern Britain."

"Florida," Irving said, getting up and trotting over to the bookshelf where the slides were stored. "That's right up your alley, Marshall."

"What?" Alice said. Fabia gave Marshall a puzzled but penetrating look.

"In fact," Irving blithely continued, beginning to switch off the lights in the room, "that motel at Coral Gables—the one Mother and I put up at—I'm next to dead certain I've got a couple of views of it here."

"You never told me you were planning to go to Florida," Alice said in the dark. "What a horrible idea. Or was it your plan to skip town and leave me with a quarter of a ton of coal and a fine-tooth comb? I suppose Fabia has known all about this for weeks."

"You're always complaining about having to stay home," Marshall began lamely.

"Oh my foot," Irving Kelso said in sincere tones. "Have I gone and given away your surprise? Fabia, would you mind turning on that lamp for a moment. No, that's all right—keep turning. There's a bulb in the socket but it's not a three-way bulb."

"Florida," Fabia said as she did so. "To take off my fur coat, lie in the sun a little, and not always worry about finding a job." She replunged the room in darkness at a signal from Irving, and soon a scene of white sand, blue sea and sky slid onto the white window shade that was serving as a screen.

"Join the waves," Alice mysteriously punned. Mrs. Kelso laughed loudly. Irving followed suit a moment later.

"Isn't that the famous Bok Singing Tower?" Fabia asked Irving.

"No," Mrs. Kelso said, "it's part of the Rollins College campus."

"Of course we intended to ask you to come along," Fabia said to Alice. "Mummy and Daddy would never let me go without a chaperon."

"If that's your idea of a joke," Marshall said. "You could hurt Alice's feelings. She feels more than she shows."

"She must feel a good deal, in that case," Fabia said quietly, and screamed. "Oh," she said, "something warm and soft just brushed against my leg."

"It must be you who doesn't like cats," Mrs. Kelso said. "Fluffy has an unerring instinct."

"Ouch," Alice said. "Now I'm getting it."

"You'd better show Fluffy the slides of himself now," Mrs. Kelso said. "He's getting impatient."

"That's a water moccasin," Irving said as the next slide came on the screen. "He's about to slip back into his black, oozy home. Sometimes this one gets a rise out of Fluffy."

"Of course, Alice, if you'd rather not come," Fabia persisted, "I suppose we could always ask Victor instead. He's been thinking of getting a job on a banana boat and maybe Key West would get it out of his system."

Marshall snickered derisively.

"Was that a laugh or a snore?" Fabia said. "Is that the Millionaire's Mile in Palm Beach, Irving?" she pursued, getting no response from Marshall.

"Could be," Irving said. "Say, I've been thinking, Marshall. I could stand a flopdown in some Grade A sunshine myself. Fabia, would you turn on the light? That's all there is, there isn't anymore, as the saying goes."

"Would anyone care for a tumbler of iced water?" Mrs. Kelso asked.

Six letters slid through the slot in the front door and lay motionless on the carpet. The cuckoo came out of its clock, surveyed the scene and retreated, having remarked on the half hour. Some minutes later Fabia Bridgewater was seen to enter her mother's bedroom. She was wearing a becomingly tailored housecoat and carrying a tray on which there was an English breakfast set and three of the aforementioned letters.

Mrs. B. ripped open the first letter, and after a brief survey of its contents, said, "Where's Victor?"

"Downstairs, I think," Fabia said, in the act of wolfing a bun. "I had a very funny dream, but I can only remember part of it."

"I wish you'd go and see where Victor is," Mrs. Bridgewater said, "because in this letter which he mailed in town yesterday, he bids good-bye to all of us."

"I'm sure I heard him reading in the living room," Fabia said, going quickly out of the room and downstairs. Mrs. Bridgewater meanwhile made the discovery that her son's bed had been slept in the previous night, though he had evidently assembled his belongings for an escape from the house.

"Fabia," Mrs. Bridgewater called from her son's bathroom, where she had just discovered traces of his whiskers lining the washbasin, "isn't that Victor out in the front yard?"

"Yes it is," Fabia called back from the living room. "Victor!" she yelled. "Yoo-hoo, Victor!"

"Your mother just phoned," Alice said. "She said for you to call her."

"Did she sound upset?" Victor asked nonchalantly.

"Why should she be?" Alice said. "Don't just stand there, help me. Can't you see I'm pulling all my hair out trying to unsnarl this curler?"

Victor leaned wearily against the sink. "I don't know why I'm never able to bring anything to a successful completion. I intended to leave home today and wrote Mother a letter yesterday saying I was. But it got so cold during the night that I decided to wait till this morning, and the mail came before I was out of the house. It hardly seems worthwhile to go through with it now."

Alice stopped patting her hair and grabbed his arm. "Listen, Victor," she said, "I've got a wonderful idea. I'm coming with you and I've got it all worked out. Sit down first and I'll give you some lunch."

"I just had breakfast. You eat something though. No, the thing is, I'd sort of given up the banana boat idea. I was planning to hitchhike up to the Adirondacks and stay in a cabin a cousin of mine has up there until I get my bearings. I'm afraid you'd find it kind of primitive."

"I'm sure I would," Alice said, advancing testily toward the refrigerator. "You know you can't just keep running away."

"I don't see why," Victor said sulkily. He refused to look at the dish of scalloped potatoes Alice set in front of him.

"Be sensible," Alice said. "Sooner or later you're going to have to think about earning a living. Now I have several ideas for how I would make money if I lived in New York."

"I couldn't stand living in New York," Victor said.

"For instance," Alice went on, "it is very easy to learn to do silk screen. We could do a line of greeting cards of unusual design and distribute them through bookstores and specialty shops."

"Where would I fit into this?" Victor asked. "Not that I'm interested."

"I wish you wouldn't talk like Fabia when she isn't around. You don't when she is. Even if I do all of the designs myself, I'm going to need someone to help with the printing, promotion, distribution and bookkeeping."

Victor choked on the scalloped potatoes he was eating. "Bookkeeping! I'm not going to do any bookkeeping. What do you think I got out of going to college for?"

"Oh all right," Alice said, "you can be the delivery boy. In fact I don't know why I mentioned any of this to you in the first place."

"It's awfully cold in here," Victor said. "You know, before I thought of going to the Adirondacks, I was going to go to New York and take some aptitude tests. They're very helpful in showing you where your real talents lie and in preventing you from getting into the wrong field."

"Who do you think is going to finance all this?" Alice asked.

"I've got some money put by," Victor said. "Not much, but enough."

Fabia came in without knocking. "Victor, I want to speak with you privately," she said.

"Aw, cut it out, Sis," Victor said. "Alice knows all about it anyway."

"Why did you run out of the yard when you heard me calling you?" Fabia asked.

"You didn't mention that part of it," Alice said.

"It's not that I disapprove of your running away," Fabia said. "Heaven knows, I would too if I had the chance."

"Shucks," Victor said. "Two against one is no fair in any man's language."

"Do you want some lunch, Fabia?" Alice asked.

"No, I just had breakfast. Besides, I'm thinking of dieting. Oh, well, just a spoon of scalloped potatoes and a bit of that meat loaf."

Alice heaped a pink willowware plate with scalloped potatoes and two slices of meat loaf and set it down in front of Fabia.

Victor looked restive. "How's Mother taking it?" he asked.

Fabia waited until her mouth was no longer full, and then said, "She seemed rather calm about the whole thing. After all, it's not so unusual for a man of nearly nineteen to leave home."

"Please," Victor said. "No editorializing. Just describe the events as they happened."

"Besides," Fabia said, "you haven't even gone anywhere yet."

"I wish I could remember exactly what day it was Marshall baked this meat loaf," Alice said.

43

"Do I hear someone maligning my cuisine?" came a familiar voice from the front hall. Marshall shepherded Dr. and Mrs. Bridgewater into the room.

"We seem to have arrived just in time for elevenses," Mrs. Bridgewater said.

"Ah," Dr. Bridgewater said, "here you are, Victor."

chapter four

"I'm disappointed," Fabia said. "I expected the sea to be bluer. I know it's quite blue, but I expected it to be even bluer."

And indeed, both sky and sea grew pale beside Irving Kelso's shirt, on which azure and indigo nightjars were at work and play. "It was certainly big of your dad," he said, "to cough up enough of the green stuff so that Victor could join us—I mean right after he got booted out of Syracuse."

"I think he thought that a nice rest away from Alice would have a settling effect on Victor," Fabia said. "Though I could have told him at the time Alice doesn't take her cello lessons all that seriously."

"Apropos, isn't that Victor and Alice standing under that

palm over there?" Irving asked. "Who is that woman with them—I can't see."

"It looks like that awful Mrs. Greeley," Fabia said. "From home."

"The next voice you hear," Irving laughed, "will be Fluffy's. Say, they're certainly taking their time with those planter's punches. We're never going to get to take that tour through the Everglades at this rate."

"Did Marshall forget to tell you? The Everglades tour is an all-day affair."

Meantime, Mrs. Greeley was saying, "We're—Abel and I, that is—at the Connolly Towers. Abel would like so much to see you, Victor, I know. And you too, Alice."

"Will do," Victor said. "Is it coral snakes whose bite kills instantly?"

"Why do you want to know?" Alice asked.

"Because we're in Florida, the home of the coral snake, the cottonmouth and the barracuda," Victor said.

Mrs. Greeley shuddered. "I'm glad Abel isn't interested in biology," she said. "He's seen six movies in the three days we've been here."

Victor stopped emptying sand out of his tennis shoes. "What ones?" he asked.

"*Rashomon, Gate of Hell, The Baker's Wife, The Day the Earth Stood Still, Johnny Guitar*, and *Mädchen in Uniform*," Mrs. Greeley said. "He's been doing handstands all morning because this weekend the Fine Arts is showing a Magnani double bill—*The Honorable Angelina* and *The Bandit*."

Victor gazed about him. "It sure gets dark early down here," he said.

"The Tropics," Mrs. Greeley said, with the air of an Old China Hand. "My regards to all—and remember, do give us a ring." But she showed no sign of leaving. "Isn't that your sister over there on the terrace, Victor?" she asked. "Who is that distinguished gentleman she seems to be having drinks with? Ought we to join them? Perhaps to say hello?"

"You're not allowed on the patio terrace in your bathing suit," Alice said. "Of course, *you* could go."

"Well, I wouldn't want Fabia to think I was avoiding her," Mrs. Greeley said, drifting purposefully toward the terrace.

"How about taking a walk down to the docks before it gets dark?" Victor suggested. "Maybe there's a banana boat in."

"No," Alice said. "Not in my bare feet. I hate looking at boats anyway. I want to change and finish my daily stint of *Anna Karenina*."

"Are you still reading that?" Victor asked. "Do you always go swimming without a bathing cap?" He eyed her lank locks.

"Of course, stupid. I want my hair to get caked with salt. Then it will look streaky and blonder when we go home. On second thought, I don't think I will read now. I'd like some brick ice cream—the kind that comes in three flavors, you know."

Victor's sun-reddened face brightened at the suggestion. "Okay," he said. "Meet you in the Crocodile Room in fifteen minutes."

"Oh, I'm not going there," Alice said. "It's too modern and garish. I'm going to that place we passed this morning, with the ceiling fans. It's like a real old-fashioned drugstore."

Victor shrugged his assent. "How will I find it?" he asked.

"That's easy," Alice said. "It's right *on* Ponce de León. It's called 'Gregg's Pharmacy.' "

Approximately one half hour later they were resting their bare forearms on the chilly marble top of a soda fountain. Overhead, the picturesque old fans drove the air in sullen wise.

"You know," Alice was feverishly whispering, "if you set it all up in New York—a real old-fashioned soda fountain—it would create a sensation."

"Excuse me," the man behind the counter said, "but this

pharmacy could never be duplicated today. You see those globes full of colored water? They stopped making them in the middle thirties. My father bought those around nineteen ten. This fountain is made of Carrara marble. People nowadays aren't interested enough to import it."

Victor was visibly shaken. "I thought Carrara marble was white," he said.

The man frowned. "Many people think that," he said. "It comes in all colors of the rainbow "

Alice smiled kindly at the grizzled man. "I think you are confusing Carrara marble in particular with all marbles in general."

Victor's face betokened relief at having one of the few facts of which he was in certain possession restored to its place.

"What about those fans? Do they still make them?" Alice asked with a condescending smile.

"Yup," the man said. "The fan factory is about a block and a half from here. You probably want to hurry up and finish and go take it in."

"I wish those wire chairs weren't such a cliché," Alice said to Victor. "Still, if we opened a soda fountain people would expect to see them in it."

Victor, whose face had gotten very red, began to whistle "Marching Through Georgia" loudly. The man turned to wait on a pretty blonde woman who spoke with a French accent.

"Oh, for Pete's sake, Victor," Alice said. "Stop whistling."

"I would like a tuna fish salad sandwich on rye toast and a glass of mineral water," the woman said, glancing at Victor whose whistling grew louder. Tired of the marching air he had switched to "Je suis Titania."

"*Voulez-vous me passer le sel, s'il vous plaît,*" Alice said to the woman.

"*Comment?*" the expensively turned-out dish said in sincere bewilderment when she realized it was she who was addressed.

"She said, will you please pass the salt," Victor said, reaching in front of her and doing same.

"Oh, I'm sorry," the woman said, "I didn't see it. Here— would you like the pepper too?"

"Certainly not," Alice said sharply, carefully sprinkling salt onto the melon but not onto the ice cream that nestled in its center.

"I have a pen pal in France," Victor said. "In Limoges."

"What strangeness," the woman said, opening her elaborately made-up eyes very wide. "I too am of Limoges. Or at least, I sometimes as a child passed my Easter vacation there, visiting my great aunt, a Limousine."

Victor laughed heartily. "I hope she has fog lights," he said. "My pen pal is named Paul Lambert," he went on. "It's a name that can be either English or French. I always planned to go visit him and stay with his folks. But that's a lost cause now. You see I was recently expelled from college."

"Oh," the Frenchwoman exclaimed. "You wealthy, irresponsible Americans." Now it was Alice's turn to laugh heartily.

"Have you been here for a long time?" Victor asked.

"I am here many times," the woman said. "Always for short periods. Since you do not, permit me to introduce myself. Claire Tosti. No, I am not related to the famed composer," she added with a little laugh.

"Victor, we're going to be late for the movies if you don't hurry up," Alice said. "They're showing *Bitter Rice* and *Tight Little Island* at the Fine Arts tonight," she explained to Claire.

Claire wrinkled her nose in distaste. "I," she said, "care only for the films of Abel Gance. Are you acquainted with his epical *Napoleon?* In France we have a film society where they show only old films," she added.

"Claire," Victor said with an unexpected show of suavity, "I

49

would like you to meet Miss Alice Bush. My name is Victor Bridgewater. We are both from Kelton, New York."

"I'm very pleased to meet you," Claire said.

The man behind the counter, galvanized from the torpid attitude in which he had been listening to this conversation, said: "Kelton, New York! Do you know some people up there name of— I can't think of their name right now. She's an average-sized woman with gray hair. He's taller but more on the thin side—but not what you'd call skinny."

"The Ralstons," Alice said. "They live near the station."

Their interlocutor laughed maliciously. "Never know it from the airs they put on down here."

"The neighborhood of the station is quite a desirable one," Alice explained. "All of the older homes are to be found there."

"You Americans have such quaint ideas of time," Claire said. "In France I live in a house that is four hundred years old."

"So what," Victor said. "The kitchen in her and her brother's house was built in sixteen fifty-two."

"Or earlier," Alice said. "That's simply the date in the hearth."

"What excites me about America is the modern architecture," Claire said. "Have you been in the Crocodile Room?"

"I'm nuts about the place," Victor said. "Sometimes Pancho lets me play the marimba. What say we get up a party and go tomorrow night? You, me, her, her brother, my sister and Irving Kelso."

"Who is Irving Kelso?"

"He is from New York City and works in her brother's office."

"It sounds enchanting," Claire said. "May I bring my friend along?"

Victor's face fell, and Claire laughed. "I tease you," she said. "There is no friend. I accept with delight."

"Fellow made me a pretty good offer for those chairs," the man behind the counter said. "I said no, but he'll be back."

A figure wearing Bermuda shorts and a pith helmet entered the store. "Give me a bottle of your deadliest poison," it said to the man behind the counter. "Oh, hello, everybody." It was Marshall.

"Is this the businessman from New York City?" Claire asked amid the laughter that had ensued.

"What's the pith helmet for?" Alice asked. "These aren't the desert sands of Libya, you know."

"It's for the rain," Marshall said.

The hostess came forward to meet them across the slippery floor. "Good evening," she said brightly. "You know," she went on, addressing Fabia, "they say it's the largest rainfall within a twenty-four-hour period since the weather bureau was opened."

"Hunh," Marshall said. "There's the rest of our party."

In the blue light that fell from a cellophane coconut, Claire was explaining to Irving Kelso, "My work as a *voyageuse de commerce* in perfumes necessitates these innumerable transatlantic trips."

Alice was staring moodily at Victor who was staring at Claire.

"Odd," Irving said. "I would have taken you for a professor. Or that woman who wrote that book about her parents who discovered radium."

Fabia rested one hand lightly on Irving's shoulder. "Eve Curie," she remarked, "is a brunette, not a blonde. Good evening. I'm Fabia, Victor's sister."

"Oh, hi, everybody," Victor said.

"*Enchantée*," Claire said. "Mlle. Curie is also old enough to be my mother."

"No, I didn't mean the mother," Irving said, "the one who actually discovered radium."

Overhead the tropic rains thundered on the sliding roof which was, of course, closed.

"You mean this is the table you *reserved?*" Alice asked Marshall. "How do you expect me to see through that pillar?"

"Please take my place, Alice," Fabia said.

"And you sit next to your brother?" Alice said. "Where's the point of coming to Florida in that?"

"You can sit here in a minute," Victor said. "I think Pancho is going to ask me up to play the marimba."

"In that event," Marshall said, "I'll ask Mlle. Tosti to dance—before the music grows too esoteric for my feet."

"You probably never heard of some of the crazy dances we do," Fabia said, "like the rhumba. But Marshall is a wonderful teacher."

"The rhumba, the mambo, the cha-cha-cha," Claire said, throwing up her arms in a gesture frighteningly reminiscent of Marta Eggerth. "What dance ever can replace the *valse!*" She left her place, and shortly she and Marshall, forehead to forehead, were going through some skilled Latin maneuvers.

Fabia pretended to admire the gladioli on the table. "Who is this *soi-disant* French woman?" she asked Irving.

"I could do with a bite," Alice said. "May I see the menu—the food menu?"

"The waiter will be with you in a moment," the hostess said. "They say the damage in the Everglades alone is already running into six figures. One alligator farmer was completely wiped out."

"I, too, often feel the pangs around this hour," Irving said. "Although I am rarely up so late—what with the office and all."

"How is the abalone steak provençale fixed?" Alice asked

the waiter, who had appeared with a sheaf of card-table-sized menus.

"As prepared by my mother," Irving said, "it contains many of the ingredients of a salade niçoise."

"You'll find a complete description on the back of the menu," the waiter said. "The breaded veal cutlet is very good tonight."

The Latin rhythms suddenly ceased. When he reached the table, Marshall chuckled as though at a familiar sight. "Tying on the feed bag, eh, Alice?"

"*Quelle excellente idée!*" Claire murmured, as though to herself. "Dancing always makes me hungry. Do you have the cassoulet toulousain tonight?" she asked the waiter.

"Only on Thursdays," was the grim reply.

"I'll have whatever everyone else is having," Alice said, "and another of *these*"—she indicated the coconut before her, from which emerged two peppermint-striped straws.

"That's a good idea," Irving Kelso said, addressing the still-frowning waiter. "And while you're at it, bring me another Dubonnet on the rocks."

As abruptly as the dance had abated, so did the drumming of the rain. "Perhaps instead of sitting here gorging ourselves," Fabia said in a clear, definitive tone, "this would be a wise moment to scoot."

"How would a cup of hot coffee strike you?" Marshall asked.

"I have a feeling there's a lot of good lurking in Claire," Victor said, eyeing the flooded though sluggish stream.

"Lurk is the word," Alice said. "Say—don't you think Captain Hanson is kind of a funny name for an Everglades guide?"

"You mean the captain part or the Scandinavian last name?" Fabia asked with a brisk little yawn. "Isn't that a drowned

53

alligator over there? Next to that mangrove tree, I mean," she finished petulantly for no apparent reason.

"To your left," Captain Hanson said, "you will see a drowned female alligator—another result of the recent storm. Since it is the mating season, this is especially tragic." He spoke with a marked Hoosier accent.

"I guess the flood was too much of a good thing for the alligators," Alice said.

"I look," Claire Tosti said, "I look—and all I see is a succession of the costliest pumps and handbags."

"Dead or alive," Captain Hanson said, "these alligators are the property of the state of Florida."

Claire emitted a piercing shriek that immobilized the other passengers of the *Maid of the Marshlands*.

"That friendly chap you see in the water ahead," Captain Hanson explained, "is a puff adder. Not the sort I'd care to run into on a dark night."

"We have no poisonous water snakes in Europe," Claire said, *"Dieu merci."*

"Wow!" Victor ejaculated. "He's a real beauty."

"Next treat—a small shower of coral snakes." Alice's lowered tone seemed accompanied by a distant cello.

"Or a boa constrictor," Fabia said, "except they're not poisonous, are they?"

"I'd be the last to complain of that," Captain Hanson replied tartly. Turning to Claire, he said, "Actually copperheads have been reliably reported in certain areas of Languedoc and the Limousin."

"The common viper, yes—the copperhead, definitely no. But what is this, Captain Hanson, that sweeps above our heads—its name, I mean?"

"It's called Spanish moss," replied the captain, "although it too is a native of the Western Hemisphere."

"I suppose it was Marshall," Alice said, "who thought up those reports that seemed so urgent all of a sudden."

"I, too, Alice," Claire said, "would be happy for their company. It is true—we women depend much on men."

Even in the gloom, Victor could be seen to blush hotly.

"On your left," Captain Hanson said, "is an awesome and spectacular grouping of mangrove trees, in which some have seen a resemblance to Chartres Cathedral."

"It is true!" Claire exclaimed. "I see it clearly and I know it well."

Their craft had entered a particularly remote and gloomy portion of the Everglades. Captain Hanson pointed out that, though the sun of noon stood overhead, scarcely a beam penetrated the massed branches. A short while later, they rounded a bend and a fawn or young deer was momentarily disclosed, standing on a hummock.

"I guess you folks have all read *The Yearling* by Marjorie Kinnan Rawlings," Captain Hanson said. "But I wonder how many of you know *South Moon Under*, her greatest work."

"Yes, it has been translated into French," Claire replied. "But I prefer the novels of Mary Webb. Tell me, Captain, is it not true that the Seminoles live not in tents—tepees?—but in some other form of dwelling?" She smiled in the way that best brought out her resemblance to the actress Viviane Romance.

"I never saw one yet that would be caught dead in a tepee," the captain replied ominously. "Most of the ones around here prefer mud, adobe or even wooden huts—but the local boozer is where you're most likely to find them."

"Please stop," Fabia said to Alice, who was humming "Chloe" and drumming her fingers on the gunwale.

Captain Hanson turned startled eyes upon them. "Stop here! It's as much as your life's worth—especially if night should fall as, indeed, it must."

"Perhaps we ought to think about heading back to the stockade," Alice said, eyeing a live alligator uneasily as she resumed her rendition of "Chloe."

"Where is Abel this afternoon?" Marshall asked Mrs. Greeley. Something in his tone indicated that he was interested less in her reply than in forestalling any questions she might wish to ask him.

"At the *Godzilla* rerun, of course. Is anything the matter, Marshall? You seem somewhat perturbed."

"I thought he'd seen it three times," Marshall continued, undaunted.

"He has," Mrs. Greeley said, "but the only alternative is *Potemkin* and *October* at the Fine Arts, and he's seen them oftener still. Where are the others this afternoon?"

"Frankly, Mrs. Greeley, they are on a tour of the Everglades and I expected them back some time ago. By 'they,' I mean Fabia, Alice, Victor, Mlle. Tosti and a certain Captain Hanson, their guide."

"Oh, I wouldn't worry," Mrs. Greeley laughed. "Those guides know their business, although I've never heard of the one you just mentioned. By the way, who is that Mlle. Tosti?"

"I think Abel could tell you more about that then I can. Have you seen Irving Kelso anywhere about? He has a way of drifting off on his own that many might find irritating. I do, at any rate."

"Hmm, so that's why Abel has been delving into the works of Colette this last week," Mrs. Greeley continued on her previous note of high spirits. "I had no idea he had an elderly admirer."

Marshall, on the point of saying, "Colette who?" said instead, "A lot depends on what you mean by elderly."

"Hi-de-ho," Irving Kelso said as he joined them. The sun

had given his skin an unappealing resemblance to a late Renoir. "Say, remind me never to take one of Abel's suggestions again," he said, pleasantly, to Mrs. Greeley. "That was the most boring movie I ever saw, except for the Odessa Steps sequence, of course."

Before Mrs. Greeley could reply, as she was obviously about to do, Marshall said, "What about the others? Or have you already given them up as so much 'gator bait?"

"Oh, they're over in the Flamingo Pit. Alice seems quite cross with you. I don't know why."

"Perhaps I can explain that," Abel said, suddenly appearing from around a corner. "Alice says that it's all your fault they were lost for two hours in an alligator-infested swamp. Claire seemed very angry about it, too, especially when I told her that Irving was at the movies this afternoon."

"Oh golly," Irving said.

Mrs. Greeley got a good hold on Abel and said, "Come along, dear; let's go over to the Flamingo Pit. I'm most anxious to meet your new friend."

"I think we shall all travel there together in a body," Marshall said.

As they reached the Pit, Claire was on the point of leaving. She laughed and said, "I'll be back as soon as I have put this antivenin kit back in my traveling case."

Although the orchestra had just begun to play "Media Luz," Alice's voice was clearly audible against it. "Waiter, bring four more chairs. On second thought, push these two tables together." However, she gave no further sign of having recognized the new arrivals.

"You'd hardly believe," Irving said to no one in particular, "how quickly we got through those reports: jig-time."

"I daresay I wouldn't." Alice said. "Oh. This is Captain Hanson."

"Pleased to meet you," the latter said solemnly. "And is this Mrs. Kelso?" he continued on a more amiable note to Mrs. Greeley.

"By no means," Mrs. Greeley said. "And you, Victor, how have you been bearing up?"

chapter five

"I'm sorry," Fabia said to the man who stood before her, "but Mr. Kelso is out of town this week—at the Mills. Perhaps Mr. Bush could help you."

"I don't know," the man said. "I just want to see somebody in Production. If Mr. Kelso can't help me, maybe Mr. Bush can."

"I'm ringing Mr. Bush now," Fabia said. "Betty, there's a Mr. Hofstetter here to see Irving. He says he has an appointment. I see," she said, and replaced the phone. "Please sit down—Miss Burgoyne will be with you in a moment. Exactly how do you spell Hofstetter?"

"Two *t*'s," the man replied after a few moments' hesitation. "Is Miss Burgoyne in Production?"

"This way," a voice—Miss Burgoyne's—unexpectedly said. Mr. Hofstetter looked about him, then scrambled to his feet.

"Love your suit," Fabia apparently called after him, though actually addressing Miss Burgoyne. The latter responded with a shrug just before disappearing around a partition, and Fabia returned her attention to *Six Characters in Search of an Author*. After a bit Miss Burgoyne reappeared, carrying her bag. "I've had my calls switched out here. Those two are good for twenty, thirty minutes," she said, pulling up a chair. Fabia carefully marked her place with a subscription blank from the Classics Club. "The tweed alone must have cost a mint. It's Donegal, isn't it?"

"No," Betty said, producing a pack of cigarettes. "It was loomed on the Isle of Mull."

"Is that one of the Shetland Islands?" Fabia asked.

The elevator gave a little click, and the pack of cigarettes swiftly returned to Betty's bag. A heavyset man in a gray herringbone Chesterfield emerged. "Well, well, Miss Burgoyne," he said. "Helping to break in the new member of the team? Welcome aboard, Miss Bridgewater." He vanished through an important-looking door.

"That's Mr. Cortland," Betty said. "He's being kicked upstairs to the international division. He's a full-blooded Cherokee Indian."

"Marshall often remarks, I suppose," Fabia said, "that he's the only true American in the firm."

"Why, yes—how did you know?" Betty replied in tones of genuine stupefaction.

"It's one of his pet hobbyhorses. Here," Fabia said producing an ashtray from a drawer in her desk. "I don't like to leave it out where it encourages people like that Mr. Hofstetter to stand around looming over me."

"You'd be surprised at some of the people who wander in and out of this office," Betty said. "The girl who had your job before used to complain about it a lot. There was one messenger in particular—an old man who wasn't quite right in the head, although perfectly harmless. He used to bring her presents wrapped up in newspaper. Once he brought her part of a coffee percolator. Another time it was an old broken-down Christmas-tree stand."

"And what happened to her?"

Betty laughed dryly. "She's Mr. Cortland's personal secretary. I'm afraid the popular view of office life is often the right one."

"Marshall tried to dissuade me from taking this job because he said there's very little opportunity for advancement."

"There's a lot that goes on around here you won't hear about from Mr. Bush," Betty said, and fell silent.

"What are you doing for lunch?" Fabia asked.

"I'm relieving you. Usually one of the girls from the typing pool does it, but they've got in a lot of temporaries because of this bug that's going around."

"Well, in that case I'll just order a sandwich," Fabia said to herself. "Possibly I'll do a little window shopping."

"How's your brother getting along?" Betty asked, *mine de rien.*

"Victor hasn't got much going for him, as they say, though people who don't have to live with him seem to find him attractive. What do *you* think?"

"Handsome is as handsome does, I always say."

"Precisely."

"He and Mr. Bush's sister seem to see quite a lot of each other."

Marshall and Mr. Hofstetter, both dressed for the outdoors, came through the door. "Perhaps one of you girls wouldn't mind taking over in there," Marshall said, his eyes fixed on the cigarette butts in the ashtray. "I'm out to lunch—no matter who calls."

"Gee—am I late?" Victor apologized, as he hastened up Professor Scott's front walk.

"Not at all," Alice replied from the porch, shifting her cello to one side. "My lips are always blue with cold."

"You could have waited inside," Victor mumbled.

"The temperature is about one degree warmer out here," Alice said. "Well, are we going to look at that store?"

"Well—yes," Victor said. "We worked it out this way. First we'll go to your house and leave the cello. Then when we're there, we'll call Mrs. Greeley and tell her to meet us at the store."

"Oh, sure," Alice said. "I certainly wouldn't want *her* standing and freezing in an unheated store."

"The electricity is turned off," Victor said, as though lost in thought. "I hope it won't be too dark to see the place by the time we get there, but I guess it won't be."

As it developed, Mrs. Greeley was not really very late but it was enough to throw her off her stride. "Oh, dear—what a morning it's been," she said placatingly to Alice, flourishing a large flashlight.

"That's all right—we can really see quite well," Alice said. "Who was occupying this place before—a motorcycle club?"

"The owner says he's willing to repaint," Mrs. Greeley said, "and make certain repairs. But any—er—modernization would have to be at your own expense."

"This wiring dates from the McKinley era," Alice mused.

"What are the sanitary arrangements?" Victor said with unexpected authority.

"There are none," Mrs. Greeley said. "However the previous tenant worked out an amicable understanding with the optometrist who has the office above. I'm sure you could do the same."

Alice took a tape measure from her bag and began calculating various distances.

"You really should see it in the daytime," Mrs. Greeley said, "in order to appreciate it fully. Now this radiator is entirely functional." The beam of her flashlight revealed a large and terribly contorted object from which, a moment later, there shot a jet of steam.

"We could fit in a counter in front of that door," Victor said to Alice. "Except then the door would have to be condemned. Maybe we could substitute a beaded curtain."

"And disguise me as Jeanne Eagels. Be careful, Mrs. Greeley, I think you're standing next to a big hole in the floor."

Mrs. Greeley inched carefully away. "I know it isn't any of my business," she asked lamely, "but what were you planning to use this place *for?*"

Alice looked at her searchingly. "What we have in mind," she confided, "is something along the lines of the old-fashioned notions shop, brought up to date."

"Oh, good," Mrs. Greeley said. "I do hope you'll have imprinted greeting cards of an uncommercial sort."

"That might come later," Victor said. "First of all we'd sort of have to see how the land lay."

"We were thinking more of old-fashioned articles," Alice said. "Like darning eggs and so on."

"Any lease, I suppose, would have to be in your name, Alice," Mrs. Greeley said, "since you, Victor, are under age."

"Whereas I," Alice said, "am as old as the hills."

"You see, the owner had some unfortunate luck with the previous tenant," Mrs. Greeley continued complacently. "He said he was opening a model agency. I don't have to tell you

63

how *that* turned out. He's just lucky none of the town fathers decided to press charges."

"According to my sources," Alice said, "they were only too happy to have him go quietly."

"Well, I guess we've seen the place," Victor said, "and I have no objections, provided the price is right. The only thing is everybody walks along the other side of this street."

Alice looked swiftly askance at Victor. "Yes, that, and the unsavory reputation of the premises make this indeed the shady side of the street. Not the big bonanza it might be in more southern latitudes."

"Actually the whole area is slated for upgrading," Mrs. Greeley remarked rather coldly. "I suppose you read that the Board of Regents voted to consider building a new manual training school in the next block. They've asked an upstate architect to submit an estimate." She added more chattily, "Though as a place to sell old-fashioned notions, painted a pleasant off-white . . ."

"To me," Alice said, "off-white is just another word for gray. Maybe we should forget the whole thing," she said to Victor. "It looks like it's going to be more trouble than it's worth."

"Of course you're the ones who know your own resources best," Mrs. Greeley said, "but if I were in your shoes, I certainly wouldn't let this slip through my fingers."

"Hi, there!" a voice said from the shadows. "I'm Dr. Carlsbad from upstairs. You must be the young folks Mrs. Greeley was telling me about."

"Hi," Victor said. "I'm Victor. This is Miss Bush."

"Victor is Dr. Bridgewater's son," Mrs. Greeley interposed.

"I haven't the pleasure of knowing your dad, except by reputation of course," Dr. Carlsbad said, eyeing Victor with a notable lack of enthusiasm. "I'm glad I caught you, Mrs. Greeley. I'm afraid that merely tampering with that petcock is no solution. What's needed is a whole new unit. About this, I must be firm." An abrupt gust of steam issued from the radiator, giving weight to his words.

"Now that the owner is back," Mrs. Greeley laughed, "these little problems must once again devolve upon his shoulders. Alice and Victor, I must run and pick up Abel. Can I drop you?"

"I don't much fancy staying on here in the dark, do you, Victor?"

"Feet, do your stuff," Victor said with a loud laugh. "So long, Doc."

"Let me know if I can be of any service," Dr. Carlsbad called after the retreating trio.

chapter six

" 'Snowdrops,' " Mrs. Bridgewater said in a clear voice, " 'that come before the swallow dares.' " Dr. Bridgewater, anxiously watching Victor get the car out of the garage, held his peace.

"It was nice of Mrs. Kelso to ask us," his wife continued over the sound of something—probably a large can—being knocked over. "Though why an elderly woman like that wants to give a large supper party, I don't know. What *is* Fish House Punch?"

"Its base," Fabia said, "is tea."

"I thought that was called Artillery Punch."

"Perhaps it is."

Dr Bridgewater winced as Victor brought the car to a

squealing stop. "All aboard for the Major Deegan Expressway!" Victor called. "Kindly fasten your seat belts."

When Dr. Bridgewater had succeeded in adjusting his to his satisfaction, he said, "I will have my eye on the speedometer, Victor."

"Don't start out by discouraging him," Mrs. Bridgewater said.

In no time at all the four travelers, none the worse for wear, were alighting beneath a sparse canopy in the vicinity of Central Park. "I'm glad I didn't wear the light gloves," Mrs. Bridgewater said, looking about for signs of soot.

"Is parking permitted here?" Dr. Bridgewater asked, sternly.

"So the sign says," Victor said.

"One up for you, Sonny," Fabia said, and added, in a whisper, "*Aux armes, citoyens!*"

"I guess I should have been brushing up on my French," Mrs. Bridgewater said, as though reading her daughter's thoughts. "I can't remember anything except, '*Ainsi, toujours poussés vers de nouveaux rivages,*' and I guess it wouldn't be very tactful to mention that to Miss Tosti on the eve of her departure. Good evening, Mrs. Kelso," she said a few moments later as they entered the austerely lit foyer. "I am Diana Bridgewater and this is my husband, Dr. Bridgewater. Fabia and Victor I believe you have met? I hope we're not too early."

"Ah. Please come this way," their hostess said, indicating the only possible direction. "Irving is engrossed in the mysteries of Fish House Punch. Meantime, Fluffy is entertaining the guest of honor." As if in reply to her words, an inauspicious yowl came from a further room.

"I often miss our Tommy," Mrs. Bridgewater said. "He was what is known as a money cat."

"Sterile, of course," Mrs. Kelso said, moving quickly to the door.

"No, quite the contrary," Mrs. Bridgewater laughed, though their hostess was already out of earshot. Claire Tosti was seated at one end of a plump sofa, near an urn of gladioli with which her suit harmonized. Fluffy was nowhere in view.

"Oh, Mrs. Kelso, what will you think?" Claire said. "I am afraid I have trod on the tail of Fluffy."

"He must be sulking in the laundry," Mrs. Kelso said. "Do sit down, all of you. I'll be back."

"Do you smell something funny?" Victor said, after a moment's pause.

"Yes," Claire said, "I do. And you would be Victor's mother, whom I have so long looked forward to meeting. And this is the doctor—the Louis Pasteur, as we say."

"*Bon soir, tout le monde*," came a deep familiar voice from an alcove. "Any orders for Fish House Punch?"

"Are there any abstainers, might rather be the question," Dr. Bridgewater rejoined jocosely. "I believe there are none."

"Do they have things like this in France?" Mrs. Bridgewater asked Claire, as she accepted a frosted mug from Irving.

"Yes," said Claire, "and then again, no." A smell of cloves hung heavy in the room.

"Since this is Claire's last evening in our fair city, I decided to make it a typically American one," Irving said, somewhat apologetically. "She can have all the champagne she wants when she gets back to Gay Paree."

Claire set her mug firmly on the low table before her, and helped herself to some peanuts in a silver dish. "Are not groundnuts," she said, "an English food?"

Mrs. Kelso appeared, framed in an archway. "I've brought Fluffy back to see Claire. He says he wants to let bygones be bygones."

There was a brief struggle and Fluffy ran from the room. "Come and have some punch, Mother," Irving said.

"I don't know what's keeping Alice and Marshall," Mrs.

Kelso said. "I told them six o'clock sharp. We're also expecting a Mr. and Mrs. Turpin. He used to be the French consul in Honolulu."

"We offered to give the Bushes a ride in," Fabia said, "but Alice had some mysterious reason for wanting to be in New York this afternoon."

"Turpin," Claire said, "the name intrigues me. In many parts of the Limousin it is very common. I mean, a large family of many branches."

"I don't think these Turpins are from around there," Mrs. Kelso said, "but I can't remember where they said they are from."

"Mrs. Bridgewater and I," Dr. Bridgewater said, "have long projected an exhaustive tour of the chateau country. Unfortunately, a doctor's time can seldom be called his own."

"Though we manage to get away for a few weeks in the summer," Mrs. Bridgewater added.

"The chateau country is lovely in the summer," Claire said, "though personally I prefer it in the fall. But why don't you visit one of the less publicized vacation spots? Picardy, for instance?"

Dr. Bridgewater frowned. "My interest is not so much in the beauties of nature—we have plenty of that here—but in Francis the First and places associated with him. It would mean a lot to me actually to set eyes on the royal salamander."

Mrs. Bridgewater evidently felt her husband had gone too far. "Picardy must be nicé, too," she said. "Tell me, do roses really grow there, or is that just a myth, like the bluebells of Scotland?"

Irving's ladle paused in midair. "The bluebells of Scotland are *not* a myth."

"Be Scotland as it may," Claire said, "roses in France are grown at Grasse, in the more sensuous climate of the Midi."

"Is that where all the perfume comes from?" Victor asked.

"No, the roses are sent elsewhere." Claire looked at her cup of punch, picked it up and drank the contents. "In Cincinnati they say the veritable Fish House Punch does not contain cloves. But to each city its own recipe, *hein?*"

Irving opened his mouth to reply, but was cut short by the sound of an electric chime from the foyer. A moment later, Marshall and Alice hurried in. Alice's hair had been arranged in a startling new way.

After greetings, seating, and the serving of more punch, Fabia turned to Alice and said, "I love it! I knew you were up to more than your usual trip to Schirmer's." Alice pretended to look puzzled.

"I love it too," Claire said. "It makes you look somehow more serious."

Alice was either about to speak or to blush when the chime again sounded. Victor beamed. "Saved by the bell!"

"I'm sorry we're late, but I only just managed to rescue Alice from under the drier," Marshall was saying as a nondescript couple in their mid-fifties entered the room.

Mrs. Kelso rose to her feet and extended both hands. *"Enchantée!"* she said, *"Enchantée, enchantée!"*

"Hello," Mr. Turpin said.

Claire swooped across the room and grabbed Mrs. Turpin by a bishop sleeve. "Mady—is it really you?"

Madeleine Turpin seemed too full for speech.

"I had no idea you were in New York," Claire went on. She turned to her rapt audience. "I haven't seen her since my school days in Grenoble."

Mr. Turpin had been looking studiously at Claire. "I think I know who it is: the petite Claudine of the rue Henri IV."

"Someone has been telling tales, I see," Claire said. "It is true: I was a terrible *garçonne*—tomboy."

"Speaking of Colette," Victor said, "I finished reading *The Last of Chéri* the other day." Alice looked uncomfortable.

"Well, well, well," Dr. Bridgewater said, to which his wife added, "Isn't this exciting?"

The two Frenchwomen lapsed into their native tongue, and Fabia, turning to Irving, said, "Might I trouble you?"

"Your weesh is my command." He glanced apprehensively at the level of the punch in the bowl. "Looks like I'll have to mix up another batch—unless we eat right away, that is."

"I could certainly do with another cup of punch," Mrs. Kelso said kittenishly. "Besides," she added to Claire and Madeleine, "dinner can wait. It's just a casserole—what we call a one-dish meal."

Fabia got up and took the place Claire had vacated on the sofa, next to Alice. "You and Victor have something up your sleeve—come on, tell."

Alice shrugged. "I wouldn't mind, but you know how Victor is."

"Oh well, I bet I know what it is anyway. One of your home industries ideas."

"My lips are sealed," Alice said, "except to tell you that you're not even warm." She looked at the alcove where Irving and Victor were talking in undertones. "Come on, Irving, I'll help you stir up another kettle of this brew."

Mrs. Kelso withdrew her attention from Mrs. Bridgewater long enough to say, "Fabia, we have a new record I'm sure you'd love—'Old London Street Cries.' Or is it Alice who's the music lover?"

"If there's one thing Alice likes more than a catch," Marshall said, "it's a glee."

"My one remaining ambition is to visit the Opéra Comique in Paris," Mrs. Bridgewater said to Madeleine Turpin. "Only the other Saturday Milton Cross was explaining the difference between grand opera and the ones they do there. It was during an intermission of *Manon*, and I was perched right by the set with my hanky ready."

" '*Je suis encore coquette*,' " Madeleine said, and sighed.

"Yes, that's the one," Mrs. Bridgewater said.

"How about *Louise*," Claire said. "That's the one *I* like, but *vraiment*, I would rather see a good baseball game any day than an opera."

Dr. Bridgewater allowed his rather large face to evince surprise. "In *France?* I thought baseball was strictly an American-Japanese game."

"Unfortunately you are right," Claire said. "Goodness, this punch is going to my head," she added, as Irving approached with a laden tray.

"Bottoms up, everyone," Irving advised. "One more round and the dinner bell will ring."

Marshall extended his cup. "Put some of that in here, boy," he chuckled.

"Mildred, Alice was so thoughtful," Irving said, as he trotted about filling mugs. "She insisted the casserole be taken out of the refrigerator now, or, as she pointed out, it would split when put into a hot oven."

"I hope the oven is set for two seventy-five," Mrs. Kelso said.

"Have done," Irving said.

"Are you sure it wasn't the thermostat you set?" Alice said in an aside. "I'm roasting in here."

"I don't think it's the thermostat, I think it's the punch, but I'll check," Irving said.

Alice looked away, humming to herself. Mr. Turpin's ears rose like a rabbit's.

"The Elgar cello concerto, surely," he said.

"No, Boccherini's. Are you fond of music?"

"My wife and I have a small record collection," Mr. Turpin said. "Mostly basic stuff, with a few frills. Elgar is one of our favorites," he added in a slightly reproachful tone.

A light of kinship gleamed in Alice's eye. Before she could

speak, something like an explosion shook the room. It was the bagpipes of the Ayrshire Rifles. A general rush to the dining room ensued.

"Women and children first," Irving cried as he whisked the lid from a steaming casserole.

"A New England boiled dinner!" Mrs. Turpin exclaimed shrilly. "I haven't had one since we left Honolulu."

As Irving filled the plates, Mrs. Kelso made sure that no one escaped the watermelon-rind pickle or the corn dodgers with which the maid was circulating.

"What are your plans when you get back to France?" Victor asked Claire as the clouds of steam subsided.

"First I shall go to Vichy, to meet my two cousins there. We are projecting a little trip through the Massif Central. Then it's back to the sweatshops of the Faubourg Saint-Honoré."

For once Fabia unbent a little toward Claire. "Tell me," she said, "is Proust very different in French?"

"I wouldn't know," Claire said. "That is, I have never read him in English, only in French. However," she added somewhat more indulgently, "I shouldn't be surprised if there was, indeed, a great difference."

"I just got a letter from my pen pal, Paul Lambert," Victor said. "He keeps insisting that I come over for the twenty-four hours at Le Mans."

"It is true that Le Mans is not to be missed," Mady Turpin said. "There are the speed and the thrills—also the terror and the tragedy."

"Even that would pall after twenty-four hours, I should think," Alice said.

"My sister," Marshall said to Mrs. Turpin, "sometimes likes to fancy herself as afflicted with boredom."

"While my brother," Alice said, "would prefer to see me afflicted in some other way."

73

"It's Marshall who's the bored one," Victor said *sotto voce* to Mr. Turpin. The latter shot him a startled glance and returned to his dinner.

"If you come to France, I hope you will look me up," Claire said to Victor. "I would like to show you the inside of a French home. We French are often accused of being not very hospitable, and it is true we sometimes like to keep people at arm's length—at first, that is."

"I hadn't noticed that," Fabia said in an undertone which unfortunately was clearly audible.

Claire gave what Fabia had once referred to as her sparkling burgundy laugh. "You must come to France sometime," she said, "and see."

"We may do so," Dr. Bridgewater replied solemnly. "I have long felt that my children should broaden their horizons."

"Good," Claire said. "When you have mastered the Louvre, and other notable spots, you may proceed with the provinces." To Victor she added, "Should you come in the summer, you may have the use of my season pass to the Bains Deligny."

"Is that a place to take a bath?" Victor asked.

"No, to swim—as the English say, to sea-bathe," Mrs. Turpin said in kindly tones. "This summer Mr. Turpin and I hope to be at my little farm. You must come and see the true country life. The very hogs are fed on chestnuts."

"What else do you grow on your farm?" Alice asked.

"My wife merely owns the farm," Mr. Turpin said. "She does not dig and delve."

"In the fall," Mrs. Turpin said, her voice rising excitedly, "when the chestnuts are ripe, hogs are driven up the hills. With sticks, by boys. Later, they are driven down again."

Though the others waited, this was the end of her tale.

"Is Victor really planning a European junket?" Irving asked Dr. Bridgewater. "I thought his—er, ah—commercial ventures were going to keep him tied up stateside for quite a spell."

Mrs. Bridgewater took advantage of the doctor's mouthful of corn dodger to intervene. "I think we'll cross *that* bridge when we come to it."

It seemed to Alice's immediate neighbors that she muttered something like, "Precisely," but no one could be sure that she had spoken.

"What about Fabia?" Marshall said, addressing no one in particular. "She won't get far in the four days' vacation she qualifies for this year."

Irving laughed until the tears came. "You don't mean to say," he said when he could, "that you thought our Miss Bridgewater was planning to work her way to the top, rung by rung?"

"At least you could never say I hadn't begun at the bottom," Fabia said. "The only rung I've skipped is the mail room."

"No one seems to be eating the corn dodgers," Mrs. Kelso said. "There's lots more hot in the kitchen. Did you know," she asked, turning to Madeleine Turpin, "that George Washington ate them every day of his life?"

"Fascinating," Mrs. Turpin said. She took a corn dodger and began to crumble it.

"Yes," Irving said, "Mildred is a mine of Colonial food lore. On Sunday we often have a few in to tea, and there's always a plate of freshly baked Sally Lunn or some Ole Koeks."

"Aren't they a little—how do you say, *indigeste?*" Claire said to Mr. Turpin, who pretended not to hear.

Marshall gave vent to silent laughter. "That reminds me of a story about my sister. Not so long ago as you might think, Alice thought she could clean up by baking and selling authentic eighteenth-century cookies in some Hessian soldier cookie molds we inherited. They were even supposed to be finished off with real gold leaf. Fortunately, we sampled them before we invested in the gold."

"Do you mean the gold leaf was to be put on the cookies themselves, or on the molds?"

"On the cookies," Mrs. Kelso said. "I know that recipe well. Your mistake was in not waiting a month or two for them to ripen. They become less hard and pleasantly chewy."

Alice frowned slightly. "I think you must be thinking of some other recipe," she said.

"Miss Bush! Miss Bush!" Humming loudly, Mr. Turpin leaned across the table.

"The Dvorak cello concerto, of course," Alice said. "Second movement."

"Dvorak!" Claire cried. "Only yesterday, while paying a last professional visit, I passed a house on which a plaque commemorated his stay in this city. I had not known of it before."

"I too know that plaque," Mr. Turpin said, "but I never can remember where it is."

"Neither can I," Claire said.

Alice started to fidget.

"Well, is everyone ready for dessert?" Mrs. Kelso asked. "Mrs. Bridgewater—another boiled potato?"

Mrs. Bridgewater led the chorus of praise and refusals that followed, which was cut short by a loud crash from the kitchen.

"Blast that cat!" Irving exclaimed. "I'm going to have him put to sleep one of these days."

"I'm sure it's not Fluffy's fault," Mrs. Kelso said, exiting swiftly.

From the kitchen came the sound of a broom pushing shards about the floor.

Irving gave a rather empty but well-intentioned laugh. "I guess it's a good thing," he said, "that there's always some Neapolitan brick in the freezer."

Mrs. Kelso reentered the room, patting her hair into place. "I'm afraid the baked Alaska is no more," she said, "but luckily I made two pies for my reading club, which meets here tomorrow. You have your choice of rhubarb-raisin or black bottom." She lifted her gaze above the heads of the diners. "I may say that Rhoda has completely exonerated Fluffy."

"Oh, Mildred," Irving said, "I *am* sorry."

"Of course." She seated herself as Rhoda Peevey entered, bearing pies.

"Isn't black bottom also a dance?" Madeleine mused.

"I shall never get used to your culinary ways," Claire said, "which are not ours, *mais enfin* . . ."

"I have tried the one," Mr. Turpin said, "and now I would like to try the other." He cleared his throat. "To me, there is one great tragedy of the past century, and it is this: that the Channel tunnel remains undug. The advantages of thus connecting the two most forward-looking countries of Europe are obvious. You may argue that it would prove a threat in time of war, but I say, nonsense. A single charge of gelignite would effectively close it."

"As an unrepentant Anglophile," Irving said, "I'd be just as glad to have 'this sceptred isle' remain a separate entity, though I don't mean to offend our French friends."

"Besides," Victor said, "hasn't it been proved that a bridge would be cheaper?"

"My dear young man," Mr. Turpin gravely said, "a bridge that could withstand the tides of *la Manche* would soon supplant the seven other wonders."

Claire gazed thoughtfully at her fork, which bore a fragment of rhubarb-raisin pie. "I sometimes wonder if boats isn't the best solution, after all." She replaced her fork on her plate.

Mrs. Peevey, puffing a little, passed through the dining room carrying a heavily laden tray. A few moments later she appeared in the door to the hall. "The coffee is in there," she said, and returned to the kitchen.

"Shall we?" Mrs. Kelso said, rising to her feet.

"I don't want to sound like an old flatterer," Mr. Turpin said to Mrs. Kelso as they proceeded toward the living room, "but I think I speak for the assembled throng when I say that your reading club's loss is our gain. Tell me, what book are you reviewing tomorrow?"

"In truth," Mrs. Kelso said, "tomorrow I merely play the hostess. A Mrs. Burke is going to tell us about her trip through some famous camellia gardens in the Carolinas. The interest of our group is not exclusively in books."

Dr. Bridgewater noted the unseemly way in which Victor grabbed the seat next to Alice. "Say," Victor muttered, "what about sets of unmatched after-dinner coffee cups?"

"Not a bad idea," Alice said, "but remember, the walls have ears."

Out of yet another of the room's mysterious recesses, Irving wheeled a tea cart on which jingled a rainbow of liqueurs and cordials. "To cap an authentically American meal," he said, "I recommend the Southern Comfort. However, it is not to everyone's taste."

"Oh, no," Claire said, "you do not play that trick on me again."

Mr. Turpin settled himself uneasily on a Moroccan leather pouf. "The Izarra will do for me."

"Is your home in the Pyrenees?" Fabia asked.

"Not only is his home in the Pryenees," Mrs. Turpin interjected, "but he has written the definitive work on high-altitude cookery."

"It has yet to appear in English, however," Mr. Turpin added ambiguously.

"Is there any of that slivovitz left?" Marshall asked.

Mrs. Bridgewater rose and crossed the room to inspect the bottles more closely. "Grappa," she said. "So called, I suppose, because made from grapes. No thank you, I'll pour my own." From the available glasses she chose a brandy pony.

"Have you never thought," Mr. Turpin said, "of Hawaii? See America first is a saying, I believe, nearer to the mark than the equally famous one about Naples."

"Useless advice," Claire said. "I know America better than most Americans. How many people in this room have ever been to Tombstone, Arizona?"

"Well," Mrs. Bridgewater said, "I could tell a white lie and say I had been. In fact, I once all but was. We planned to spend a winter break in Flagstaff, and from there go on a few junkets. But as luck would have it, the high altitude gave Victor continual nosebleeds, so we were forced to beat a retreat to Biloxi, Mississippi."

"My ambition," Mr. Turpin said, "is to visit Scottsdale, Arizona, though I hear it has changed sadly in the last few years."

"America and her tragic suburbs!" Claire fetched a sigh. "However, I was somewhat relieved to learn that the population of Vermont—perhaps my favorite of the continental states —is shrinking."

"I cannot say that this fact causes me excessive joy," Dr. Bridgewater begain in heavy tones, but he was quickly interrupted by Fabia. "Do you mean, Claire, that you've been in all fifty of the United States?"

"Yes. The state that neither needs nor uses perfume has not, as you say, been invented."

"I suppose some need it more than others," said Alice, who for some time had seemed lost in thought.

Mrs. Kelso rose to her feet. For a moment her startled guests surmised that she was about to ask them to leave. "I don't believe," she said, "that you have heard Irving sing."

"I don't think it's that kind of an evening, dear," Irving said. "You know what they say about speeding the parting guest."

"What time does your plane leave?" Alice asked.

"At eleven," Claire said, "but we have to be at the airport at nine-fifteen. I suppose I should allow an hour to get there."

When you add up all the toing and froing," Mrs. Turpin said, "it's really quicker to take the boat."

"Boats are nice," Claire said, "provided one can escape one's fellow passengers, and stay in one's deck chair, reading a long old-fashioned novel. The last time I came by boat, I read most of *The Pasquier Chronicles*, by Georges Duhamel. But usually one is trapped into dancing and going to tea parties. On the whole, I think I prefer air travel. It's somehow more dynamic."

"A transatlantic flight," Mrs. Turpin said, "I find just right for the latest Simenon. Unfortunately, I am usually too nervous to concentrate."

"Marshall," Alice said, "wake up."

"I wasn't asleep," Marshall said. "You were talking about how much better it is to travel by boat than by train."

A sound of quarreling voices, half human, half feline, was heard. Irving left the room and soon returned, bearing Fluffy. "It seems," he said, "there is now no leftovers problem."

"Oh the greedy," Mrs. Kelso said. "Come here and apologize."

"Can I hold him for a while, Mrs. Kelso?" Victor asked eagerly.

As soon as Fluffy was settled on Victor's lap, he began to purr loudly. "Ow!" Victor said. "Stop that, kitty."

"He wants you to scratch him behind his ears," Mrs. Kelso explained. "Either ear."

"Oh, Victor, your dark blue suit," Mrs. Bridgewater said.

"I'm scratching, but the more I scratch the deeper in he digs," Victor complained.

"He certainly has taken to you," Mrs. Kelso said. "And his highness is very choosy about his friends."

Fluffy suddenly released Victor and began to walk along the back of the sofa. When he came to where Claire was sitting he placed a tentative paw on her shoulder, as though to test its firmness. With a practiced movement, Claire lifted Fluffy from the back of the sofa to the floor. "A hair of the dog, sometimes, perhaps; a hair of the cat, never."

"I thought the French were a nation of cat lovers," Victor said. "Anyway, that's what you'd think to hear Colette tell it."

Mr. Turpin frowned. "One could scarcely say that Colette, whatever her talents, is *typiquement française.*"

"I can well believe *that,*" Dr. Bridgewater said.

"Colette had a faithful old servant who kept her clothes brushed," Claire said to Victor. "I have no such luck."

Dr. Bridgewater, who had been fumbling ceremoniously in his clothes, produced a small red book. "Might I trouble you, Miss Tosti," he said, "for your French address?"

Claire wrote down a number with a small gold pen. "This is my office number," she explained. "My secretary always knows where I can be reached. You see, usually I am *comme l'oiseau sur la branche*—like the bird on the branch."

"What does that mean?" Alice asked.

"I think it is self-explanatory," Dr. Bridgewater said. "In any case, Mother, we ought to be thinking about returning *chez nous.*"

"Anybody like to adopt a cat?" Irving asked.

chapter seven

"It's wonderful what white paint will do for a place," Victor said.

"Especially if you put on another coat," Alice said firmly.

"Do you think the ceiling needs one too?"

"That most of all."

"What do you think we should do about the floors?"

"As a matter of fact, I've been looking into that," Alice said. "Coconut matting now comes in various dyed colors. I was rather taken by a kind of off-tomato."

"That sounds good," Victor said, "except I thought we were going to go easy on the decorator touches. You don't think that with the bentwood rocker . . . ?"

Alice shrugged.

"My, my," Dr. Carlsbad said, appearing in the doorway. "I never would have recognized this place. It looks just like a hospital. When you finish here, I could use you in my consulting room."

"I was kind of worried about its looking too hospitalish," Victor said. "But when we get in the merchandise—especially the Mexican things—I think that will perk it up quite a lot."

Dr. Carlsbad gazed around with a critical eye. "If you were worried about it," he said, "you could always paint one wall a contrasting color—maybe a deep purple." A silence ensued. "Where are the bulk of your imports coming from?"

"Well," Victor said, "you see, we're trying not to specialize —like French copper-bottomed pots, for instance. On the other hand, we are trying to play down Japan a little."

"And what's more," Alice boomed with unexpected gusto, "we feel it's time the Western Hemisphere had its day in court. Besides Guatemalan *rebozos*, we're getting some Eskimo walrus-tooth accessories and some Navajo turquoise and silver jewelry that's not the usual junk."

"Is there any central theme to all of this?" Dr. Carlsbad asked.

Victor looked sly. "You mean the figure in the carpet? That's a poser you'll have to solve for yourself."

Dr. Carlsbad laughed. "Well, I just hope the folks in the neighborhood will be able to do the same," he said. "In general they're not much given to sophistries."

"Since we're not selling cheese, Old Dutch Cleanser or bubble gum," Alice said, "we don't expect to see much of the neighbors. Victor, would you pass me that can of Spackle?"

Dr. Carlsbad seemed disinclined to abandon a fertile train of thought. "Well, I certainly admire your pluck," he said, "and I don't want to discourage you either, but it's been my experience that the local citizenry are extremely limited in their outlook. Since they've only just taken to harlequin frames, I don't see how you can expect to convert them overnight to Eskimo buttons."

"If you've got a little extra time," Victor said, "maybe you could help me heft these packing cases."

A bell was heard ringing above. "Sorry," Dr. Carlsbad said smoothly, "but I'm afraid I hear a pair of ground smoked lenses calling."

"Wouldn't you know it," Victor muttered. "I think we ought to discourage him, Alice, from dropping in too regularly—sanitary conveniences or no sanitary conveniences."

Alice looked around the shop and out into the gray street. "Personally," she said, "I'm ready to sell out to the first comer: profit no object."

"Oh, come on," Victor said. "Now that you've got something you always wanted, you could at least act a little more cheerful."

Into the discouraging view walked the figure of Mrs. Bridgewater. She was dressed in geranium wool and carried a shopping bag sprinkled with Bonwit Teller's violets.

"Goodness," she said, "I never thought I'd find you. I don't think I've ever been on this street before."

"You've been on it hundreds of times," Victor said, "to my certain knowledge. But we were always driving and you didn't notice."

"Uhmm," Mrs. Bridgewater said, as though agreeing that the street offered little enough that might catch her attention. "Here," she added listlessly, "I made both of you a sandwich. There are a couple of wedges of last night's pie and tea in the Thermos. I hope you like it pretty sweet too, Alice."

"Thank you very much," Alice said, "but you needn't have gone to so much trouble. There's a perfectly decent luncheon-ette next door. This isn't the Limberlost, appearances to the contrary."

"I'm afraid I've heard too much in my time about hepatitis, trichinosis and salmonella to be an altogether trusting person. Victor, just what did you say to your father last evening? I've been trying all morning to explain that you certainly didn't mean it in the way he took it."

Victor, about to hammer a board, straightened and removed some nails from his mouth, one by one. "I suppose he's sore because I wanted to borrow some money," he said, "and use the series-E bonds Uncle Merv gave me as collateral."

"Your father," Mrs. Bridgewater said gently, "has learned to look beyond today. And beyond tomorrow, too, for that matter. It's very nice that you're so wrapped up in your little venture, but—well—it's scarcely a life's work, is it?"

"I don't see why not," Victor said. "Besides, where would we be today if Grandpa Bridgewater hadn't opened a harness store in Paducah?" He began hammering loudly.

Mrs. Bridgewater turned to Alice, whose mouth was full of sandwich. "You can't talk to either of them. If one doesn't fly off the handle, the other does. Last night not one word was said at dinner. Fabia finally went upstairs and got a volume of Proust: then she and the doctor had words."

"Well," Alice said, swallowing harder than the bite she had taken seemed to justify, "there's no contenting some people. Marshall has been sulking lately too, although he always told me I should get out and do something. But in my experience, everybody who embarks on a new business venture is looked upon as slightly demented."

A conflict of loyalties fought it out on Mrs. Bridgewater's face before she said, "That's very true. I try to tell the doctor how unreasonable he is: he was perfectly willing to finance years and years of college for Victor, so I don't see why he won't be more generous now." She paused for a thoughtful moment. "But he'll come round. '

"Well," Victor said, "that shelf is up and I'm ready to call it a day."

"Why I'd love to, Irving," Fabia said, "but I already have a date for lunch with Betty. Unless you'd like to make it a Dutch-treat threesome?"

"Well, just this once won't hurt, I guess. But you know what they say about crowds. Seriously though, how about lunching in a Japanese or Chinese restaurant?"

Fabia had just started saying something about tempura shrimp when Marshall strode through one of the silent doors. He was as pale as his naturally high color would allow. "Well, if she isn't here, where is she?" he asked.

Fabia put down the ball-point with which she had been toying and placed her hand on the telephone. "In what way may I be of help to you, Mr. Bush?" she asked. "If you're looking for Betty," she added before he could reply, "she's down at the blood bank."

Irving, the moving spirit of the company blood bank, glanced at his watch, muttered, and headed for his office.

Marshall frowned. "I sometimes think the blood bank is stocked entirely with Miss Burgoyne's blood. At any rate, she seems to find its rituals endlessly fascinating."

"Oh well," Fabia said, "she won't be gone all that long."

"In that case," Marshall said, "perhaps you'd care to pinch-hit for her until the vampires release her. Mr. Cortland wants to dictate a letter."

"Why me?" Fabia asked. "The whole eighth floor is awash with happy helpers."

"As it happens," Marshall said, "the entire typing pool is committed to getting out the annual report." But before Fabia's typing prowess could be put to the test, Betty Burgoyne emerged smiling from the elevator.

"Let's make it an early lunch, shall we, Fabe?" she said

chattily. "Dr. Pratt told me to indulge my penchant for T-bone steaks to the hilt. Doctor's orders, you know," she winked at Marshall.

"I trust you're not feeling too anemic to answer a few calls and perhaps type a little," Marshall said.

"I can do the phone bit all right," Betty said, "but Dr. Pratt told me to avoid all physical exertion, including typing, until after lunch."

"Miss Burgoyne," Marshall said unsteadily, "you are driving me to my uttermost limit."

"Oh well, if it's that important I can do it," Fabia interjected. "I can take dictation in longhand if he doesn't go too fast. My typing, though, is strictly hunt and peck."

Marshall appeared to suffer a rush of blood to the head, but before he could speak, Betty tottered a little, steadied herself on the desk, and was led away by Fabia.

"Do you think he's really peeved?" Betty asked, after Fabia had piloted her to a day bed in the ladies' lounge.

"Well, yes, he did seem pretty peeved, even for Marshall. But I think it's Alice he's really mad at: he's afraid she's slipping through his fingers. It might be wise not to give away any more blood until this blows over."

"Is Alice still planning to open her gift shop, or is that just another pipe dream?"

Fabia glanced at her a shade reprovingly for this familiarity. "Yes," she answered, "but she and Victor have run afoul of some old zoning law that was just unearthed. It seems that all the houses have to be at least nine feet from the sidewalk, and theirs is only seven. What will happen now is anybody's guess."

Betty sighed. "It sounds just like my own experience with the farm-fresh eggs. Would you hand me that bottle of cologne? I think I'll dab a little on my forehead. I'd've thought Marshall would be relieved at this turn of events."

"Actually it's worse for him than before, because he worries about what Alice will do next, now that she's had a taste of blood . . . so to speak."

"I'm surprised he doesn't move into a bachelor flat," Betty said. "Lots of men in this office live in them."

"Oh well," Fabia said, "I wouldn't underestimate Marshall's satisfaction in being the head of a household—however small and inharmonious."

chapter eight

"I have just spoken to the concierge," Dr. Bridgewater said. "He informs me that this evening's performance of *Tartuffe* is sold out."

"Then it's *Le Soulier de Satin*," Fabia said with ill-disguised pleasure.

"That too is sold out," Dr. Bridgewater said, shading his eyes against the harsh glare from the ceiling fixture. "The only thing he has seats for is something called *Ali Baba*—a musical comedy I believe."

"Is it some kind of children's entertainment?" Mrs. Bridgewater asked plaintively. This drew a coarse and rather knowing guffaw from Victor.

"Hardly," Dr. Bridgewater said, frowning at his son. "In fact, children—those under the age of eighteen at any rate—are not allowed in."

Fabia joined Victor at the window. Outside, the rain fell ruthlessly on the Quai Voltaire, the Seine, and the greenery beyond. "I couldn't care less about that stuff," Victor said. "Anyway, I have an appointment with my pen pal, Paul Lambert."

"Just who is this person, Victor?" Mrs. Bridgewater asked. "I mean, I know you've corresponded with him through the years, but do you have any idea what his background is?"

"His father," Victor said, "is an *avocat.*"

"A lawyer—an attorney," Dr. Bridgewater explained.

"Except," Victor added, "in France there isn't anything shady about it. It's more like being a judge."

"How old is he?" Mrs. Bridgewater asked.

"In his middle thirties, I think," Victor said.

"What kind of work does he do?"

"Test sports cars," Victor continued imperturbably. "Before they leave the factory. He also drives them around to different parts of the country where there are going to be auto races."

Dr. Bridgewater sat down heavily on the side of the bed where his wife was stretched out with—as she put it—her feet up. "Is all this true, Victor? Or are you merely tormenting your mother?"

"Oh well," Mrs. Bridgewater said, crossing and uncrossing her ankles, "as long as he doesn't race them, I suppose there's no harm in it."

"*La Grande Maison de Blanc,*" Fabia said, reading the name off the side of a passing truck. "He sounds pretty horrible to me and I intend to avoid meeting him at all costs."

There was a sharp tap at the door which immediately

opened. A maid entered carrying a large basket of fruit. "*Monsieur-dame,*" she said as she withdrew.

Mrs. Bridgewater took a small envelope from the top of a pineapple and read the note inside. " 'Welcome to my country—or rather, *Soyez les bienvenus,* since you must speak French now that you are here. Please do me the honor of being my guests at dinner Thursday night. R.S.V.P. (signed) Claire Tosti.' Oh dear," Mrs. Bridgewater went on, "and it was Mrs. Kelso who had her to dinner. Still, how very thoughtful."

Fabia examined the notepaper. "Engraved," she said thoughtfully, and began to hum a little tune.

"No, Victor," Mrs. Bridgewater said, "I wouldn't eat any of that—at least not until I've had time to wash it all thoroughly."

"I'm getting sick of this claustrophibic atmosphere," Fabia said. "Why don't we take one of those boat rides along the Seine? Even Victor would enjoy that."

"In the rain?" Victor said.

"The top part is glassed in," Fabia explained patiently. "Look, there goes one now."

"I," Mrs. Bridgewater said, "am not going to budge until dinner. Who would have dreamed that a little thing like the Sainte Chapelle could be so taxing?"

"I certainly wish Alice were here," Fabia said. "She at least has some get-up-and-go to her."

"*That* she certainly has," Mrs. Bridgewater said. "In fact, I expect we'll be running into her any day now—loping along the Champs Elysées with that peculiarly aggressive gait of hers." Victor looked inscrutable.

"Wasn't that a card from Alice you got this morning?" Fabia asked him. "It looked like her writing, and besides no one but Alice would choose a view of the Chrysler Building."

At this the telephone made a loud rasping sound. Dr. Bridgewater cleared his throat, picked up the receiver and said, in his chestiest tone, "*Oui? Oui . . . Oui . . . Mon fils est ici.*" He hung up and turned to Victor. With the air of one diagnosing cancer he said, "A Mr. Lambert is coming up."

"Good grief," Victor said. "I could have met him in the lobby."

"I don't think . . ." Mrs. Bridgewater was beginning, when the door burst open. A dark heavyset man of thirty-eight, with bushy but receding hair and wearing a black suit and raincoat, advanced into the room.

"Well, Victor," he said, or rather, roared, "at last we meet!" He bore down upon the startled youth and slapped him on the shoulder with a massive paw. "And you must be Victor's parents and sister, about whom I hear so much," he added, beaming at the others.

"Well," Mrs. Bridgewater said, struggling to her feet, "this is a surprise."

"You must excuse my impatience," Paul said, "but I have been waiting so long to see Victor, to embrace him. We are pen pals, you know."

He spoke with a strong American accent, pronouncing Victor "Victer."

"Paris!" Claire said, somewhat superfluously. Under a heavy June sky, the city was looking more than usually maleficent. Mrs. Bridgewater, refusing to step out onto the balcony, gazed apprehensively at the scene from the relative safety of the living room. To the right rose the stern contours of the Ecole Militaire; on the left, the Eiffel Tower plunged into low-hanging clouds.

With a gesture that seemed likely to sweep them into the void, Paul Lambert pointed to some trees. "There," he said, "was the home of Blériot, the famous airman."

"That house there," Claire added hastily, indicating an imposing granite pile just opposite them, "belonged to Sacha Guitry.

You may not have read his books and plays, but you have probably seen his films."

"The exterior," Dr. Bridgewater said, "is François Premier, though somewhat bastardized." After a noncommittal pause, the group edged its way back into the living room.

"Oppressive, isn't it?" Claire's sister Nadia said. "The night air, I mean." In reply, a bolt of lightning lit up the park below and at once thick sheets of rain began to fall.

Dr. Bridgewater turned to her as though to the business of the day. "I understand, Mademoiselle, that you are an *antiquaire*."

"Yes," Nadia said, smiling pleasantly. "I am in the antiques business."

"Ah," Mrs. Bridgewater said. She peered about at the comfortable but apathetic furnishings of the room as though there were some point she had missed.

Nadia seemed to sense her difficulty. "Many of my clients are Americans," she continued encouragingly.

"Somehow," Fabia was saying to Claire, "I had not expected Paris to be quite so much like Florida."

"Yes," Claire said, "here, too, we have rain." She switched her attention to Mrs. Bridgewater. "I see you are admiring the Charles X prie-dieu. It unfolds to become library steps."

"How convenient," Mrs. Bridgewater said.

"Hasn't most of the good stuff been gotten to already?" Victor asked Nadia.

"Uhmmm," Nadia said, as she considered his question and the possibility of an answer, but Claire was there first.

"Styles come and go," she said, "in antiques as in all things. In fact, Nadia has launched some herself—for instance, the current rage for English brass fenders."

Mrs. Bridgewater gasped and hastily took some nuts from a dish that declared itself a souvenir of the Trocadéro.

"Remember those firedogs we saw in the window at Madeleine Castaing's?" Dr. Bridgewater murmured confidentially to his wife.

"Mme. Castaing is one of my closest colleagues," Nadia said a shade reprovingly. "Of course it was she who started the vogue for *la mode anglaise* just after the last war. And yet I find all those tartans and antlers a trifle—how shall I say?— lugubrious."

A far-off tinny sound was heard through the abating rain. Claire winked mischievously at Dr. Bridgewater. "Ah—the secret guest."

Dr. Bridgewater goggled. A moment later the maid ushered a humid figure into the room. It was Irving Kelso.

"Dr. Bridgewater, I presume?" he said with a broad grin and outstretched hand.

Everyone expressed shock, but in fact, no one was too surprised. It had appeared likely for some time that Irving would win the salesman-of-the-year award from his company, which took the form of a round-trip ticket to Paris. Even before the Bridgewaters had left New York, he had hinted darkly at running into them in Harry's Bar, or some such.

When Victor had spelled this out for Nadia and Paul, the latter asked, "And just what is it this company makes that he sells so well?" His face bore the expression of one who every now and again dips into *l'Humanité*.

"Oh what difference does that make?" Claire said. "The point is, he's here. But what—" she scanned the depths of the vestibule—"have you done with Mme. Kelso *mère?*"

Irving looked grave. "Well, you know—or I guess actually you don't—Fluffy passed away. I was really glad of this chance to get Mildred out of the apartment and away from all the associations. She's at the hotel, lying down. It was a pretty bumpy flight."

"Poor Fluffy," Claire said. "I always remember him."

There was a moment of respectful silence, in which Paul and Nadia joined with puzzled expressions, not certain that they were registering enough emotion. Finally Claire resumed her role of Mistress of Revels. "You must be parched," she said, taking a martini from a silver salver held out by the maid and offering it to Irving. "Here, try this on for size."

"But, Mr. Kelso," Nadia said, "you need not gulp. There is yet time for another wee drop."

Esperanza continued to circulate with the tray of martinis. Claire glanced at them warily, as though able to judge the degree of dryness. "How are they?" she asked of Victor, who was on his third, in tones of sincere concern. "It is the one thing we French, with all our experience of wines and cognacs, never seem to be able to do right."

"They taste fine to me," Victor said. "I like the kind of gin you get over here, or whatever it is."

"I'd like to ask you a question," Mrs. Bridgewater said to Nadia during a lull. "A friend of mine back home has asked me to bring her some old prints—something she can have framed to hang in the living room. Do you know where I could get some?"

"What kind of prints?" Nadia asked.

Mrs. Bridgewater frowned. "Her living room is done in pleasantly muted tones, with a few heirloom pieces mixed in."

Nadia smiled understandingly. "I think a few *vues d'optique* ought to fill the bill. I shall keep my eye open for you."

Meantime, Fabia was saying to Paul, "In other words, you enjoy all the excitement of a dangerous sport, without running any of the risks."

"Say, that's quite a smell coming from the kitchen," Irving said to Claire. "What is it?"

"I persuaded Esperanza to make her famous *arroz con pollo*," Claire said. "It's really the thing she does best."

At the sound of these words, Victor placed his martini glass on the piano, kicked aside a small scatter rug, and brought his heels down smartly on the parquet. "*Ole!*" he shouted. "*Ole! Ole!*"

Esperanza hastily announced dinner.

When it was over they returned to the salon. The rain had stopped, and above the dripping trees a few stars could be seen between the clouds. Claire flung open the doors to the balcony, and a gust of wind tore through the apartment. When Paul and Victor had succeeded in closing them, they rejoined the others, who were grouped around a small coal fire in a grate.

"I believe I read somewhere—perhaps in Anatole France," Dr. Bridgewater said, "that the Paris weather is as fickle as a woman."

"Actually the weather is always terrible here," Nadia said, "especially in the month of June. And we Parisiennes are faithful in our fashion," she added kittenishly.

This sally appeared to leave Dr. Bridgewater somewhat at a loss, and Claire interposed the suggestion that they go out to a nearby cabaret. Mrs. Bridgewater replied that she had always wanted to see the Lapin Agile, and wondered if it was still open. It was not so very long before they were there and seated at the best table, while a guitarist bent over Mrs. Bridgewater and serenaded her with a song from the Belle Epoque, which neither Claire nor Nadia showed much interest in translating.

"Do you travel a lot?" Paul asked Irving Kelso.

"Yes and no," was the reply.

"I don't get it," Paul said, frowning.

Irving, who was afraid he might have offended the foreigner—for so he thought of him—hastened to explain. "I mean—I'm constantly on the move between New York and

Dayton, Ohio—but I don't know if you'd call that travel. A trip to Paris, on the other hand . . ." He rolled his eyes suggestively and made a gesture traditionally associated with French chefs.

Paul nodded. "I understand," he said. "As we say here, 'It's the icing on the cake.'"

"That's funny," Irving said. "My mother often says that, though she knows no French."

"That's funny," Paul said.

Victor, whom the Beaujolais at dinner had decidedly not rendered less boisterous, downed his *cerises à l'eau de vie*, spat out the pits, and plunked his glass on the table. "*Garçon—on a soif!*" he thundered.

He received a look of brief surprise from his companions, perhaps for his unexpected command of idiom.

The waiter brought fresh drinks for everyone, though the others had scarcely touched theirs. The guitarist, meantime, had struck up a jangling lament. Turning to Nadia, Fabia murmured, "If we give him some money, will he go away?"

"I'm afraid he would be terribly offended," Nadia said. "But after the next song, he *will* be expecting a little something." Fabia relayed this to her father, and the situation was dealt with accordingly.

They did not long remain in peace, however. A grizzled octogenarian wearing a smock and beret and carrying a large pad under his arm soon approached the table with an offer to sketch Mrs. Bridgewater's portrait, and, at the doctor's insistence, did so.

Irving now began to mellow to the scene. After tugging on his drink and releasing a smoke ring, he turned to Paul and said, "Tell me, Paul—is this where the Paris artists congregate? Or is it just an act they put on for the tourists?"

Claire dipped her fingers in her drink and mischievously flicked a few drops at Irving. "Do not play the Philistine," she said. "No artists have been sighted in this district since the Bateau Lavoir sank."

"Do you find it's harder to bear your friends' little idiosyncrasies when you're on a trip?" Alice asked. "I suppose it's the same principle that makes you go out of your way to be friendly to people you'd hardly speak to at home."

"On the liner, I did have a feeling," Fabia said, "that the Bridgewater family was taking part in a revival of *Resurrection*."

Victor exhaled a puff of smoke, which was quickly wafted over the boat railing in the direction of some trees bordering the river. "These are more like cigars than cigarettes," he said. "Except you don't inhale with cigars."

"I am a veteran smoker," Paul Lambert said, "since thirteen. But I never inhale. In that way I maintain my health."

"What's the point of smoking if you don't inhale?" Victor asked.

"Sometimes I have the feeling that I've seen all this before," Alice said.

"You did—from my car, a few minutes ago," Paul said with a laugh. "Paris is a very small city," he added in a more serious tone. "You see the statue of the Zouave on that bridge? We have the habit of measuring the water level with it. When the Zouave has wet feet, the level is high."

"Is *that* the one," Victor said. "I nearly missed it."

"That street over there should make you feel homesick," Paul continued, obviously warming to his task. "It's called New York. I have an aunt who lives in it. Her name is Marie-Louise but we all call her Loulou."

"Is that the aunt who owns the Théodore Rousseaus and the Diazes?" Fabia asked.

"No. Aunt Eulalie is more a cousin of one of my grandmothers. She lives at Rennes. Well, near it."

Alice frowned. Perhaps she wished the conversation would take on a more personal character. But she said nothing.

"A *centime* for your thoughts," Victor said, resting his elbows beside hers.

Alice's frown deepened slightly, but she made an effort to overcome her annoyance. "I was just thinking about the movie we saw last night. I hated it—except for the last five minutes."

"*Esquimaux Gervais!*" Victor cried in a falsetto voice. "*Esquimaux Gervais!*" A number of people—French, no doubt —turned to stare at him.

"Do you like the French ice cream better or the American?" Paul suggested to Fabia.

"You like anything," Victor said, "that's about a woman walking down a long empty road."

"It's getting rather chilly out here," Fabia said as though in reply to Paul's question. "Shall we go in?"

Just then an unseen hand caused some klieg lights to shoot their beams up into the trees. "*Comme c'est féerique,*" Paul said in a solemn voice.

"That's a dumb remark, even coming from you," Alice said, though her tone seemed to disguise a certain admiration for Victor.

Victor spoke more confidentially. "Listen, Alice, I wish you'd tell me: what did Marshall say when you said you weren't going to the Adirondacks?"

Alice shrugged.

"Yes, we may go in if you like," Paul said. But no one seemed in a hurry to move. Without warning a rocket climbed high into the sky, where it exploded. Paul turned a complacent face to his American friends. "With the renewed interest in promoting tourism, every day is Bastille Day."

Everyone waited for another rocket, but none was forthcoming. Instead, from a loudspeaker harrowingly close at hand, there began to issue the strains of "Musetta's Waltz."

"Would anyone like a Coca-Cola?" Paul asked.

"*I'll* get them," Victor said, and went charging off.

"I wouldn't mind one of those jawbreaker ham sandwiches you seem to feature over here," Alice said. "And a glass of soda water."

With an open glance, Fabia appraised Alice's robust figure. "Don't you want to save some room for the onion soup? According to Baedeker, hearty helpings are the rule at Les Halles."

"In this country," Paul said, "it is possible to eat and eat without ever gaining any weight." Alice exhibited her profile to the night.

Victor came back with some small bottles of what appeared to be a powerful orange dye. "They ran out of Coca-Cola," he said apologetically.

"Just a minute, sir, your change, please," said a waiter who had been pursuing Victor. He seemed startled when Victor accepted it, and walked angrily away.

Alice yawned and shuffled her feet. " 'Stand close around, ye Stygian set,' " she said. Doesn't this *bateau ivre* ever dock?"

Paul looked crestfallen. "I guess boats are not much fun," he said. "Would you like to go to some nightclubs? I could take you to one in Montmartre that is frequented by gangsters."

"Anything," Fabia said, "so long as we don't wind up at another Akim Tamiroff festival. However, I am determined to visit the site of Les Funambules."

"I'm not sure I know where that is," Paul said.

"Frankly, I'd settle for a hot bath and the English weeklies," Alice said as the boat crunched to a stop next to a dock. "But—*vive l'aventure!*"

chapter nine

"It's hard to believe it wasn't built to look that way," Alice said, turning her back on the Forum. "Listen, Marshall, I want you to write to them about that furnace. I refuse to spend another winter like the last one."

"You don't seem to realize that what our tenants are complaining about is too much heat," Marshall said, wiping his brow as though in sympathy.

Around the corner of some crumbling brickwork Mrs. Bridgewater appeared. "Have you seen Fabia and Guglielmo?" she asked. But her words were lost in the roar of traffic. Alice, however, had divined her question.

"They went thataway," she said, pointing toward a hill which was crowned with trees.

Marshall glanced briefly about him, then began scattering check marks broadcast through the pages of a guidebook.

"He seems a nice enough young man, don't you think, Alice?" Mrs. Bridgewater asked.

"Oh, sure," Alice said. "Say, how about this afternoon for a nice cool catacomb?"

"He has a sister who's married to an American and lives in New Jersey," Mrs. Bridgewater continued. "Elizabeth, I think he said. The town."

Marshall closed his guidebook with a snap. "According to *The Rome Daily American*, the heat is even worse there. Where do you suppose she's dragged Irving off to now?"

"She has a insatiable appetite for *granite*. She claims there's a Southern recipe that's almost the same," Mrs. Bridgewater said.

"Did you see the card Alice got from Victor?" Marshall asked.

Alice fished in her pocketbook and retrieved it. "After waiting in line for half an hour at American Express, I was rewarded by *this*," she said.

Mrs. Bridgewater took the card. The picture on the front showed a trailer camp in a pine woods. The message on the back read, "*Saluti!* Victor," and, "*Bons baisers à toutes et à tous*–Paul."

"How thoughtful," Mrs. Bridgewater said.

"Shall we go and rescue Fabia from the Tarpeian Rock?" Alice asked Marshall. "Or are you *stanco?*"

"Look," Marshall said. In the midst of the onrushing traffic careened an open carriage in which sat Irving and his mother. Mrs. Kelso looked as though she had just pulled the name Boadicea out of a hat and was determined to see the thing through.

In a moment Irving was alighting at their feet with unusual alacrity. "Hi, folks," he said. "This gentleman" —he indicated the driver— "has promised to give us a Cook's Tour of the city for twenty dollars, tip included. We get to see the site of the nineteen forty-two World's Fair and Ostia Antica, a ruined city—like Pompeii."

"*Ostia Antica, no,*" the driver said, "*il Foro Italico, sì.*"

Irving scanned the exhaust-fumed horizon. "I don't see any sign of Fabia and that friendly native."

"We can't all fit in that," Mrs. Bridgewater said. "Besides, half would have to ride backward."

"I don't think you'd find that Cesare—that's the horse's name—moves fast enough for you to become carsick," Mrs. Kelso said. "He's quite sluggish, as a matter of fact."

"He's not the only one," Alice said.

"Would anyone like some grapes?" Mrs. Kelso said. "Dr. Bridgewater, I trust, is enjoying the congress?"

"He seems to be having a high old time," Mrs. Bridgewater said. "He has made some new acquaintances and renewed others." She lowered her voice. "I gather he finds the University of Padua of great antiquity in more than one sense. Of course he can't speak too openly on the phone."

Irving nodded. "Mother and I are keeping our fingers crossed until we get out of here," he said. "Actually we both had a touch of slight indigestion after we got back to the hotel last night. Just the usual tourist stuff."

Alice yawned and turned toward the view. In the sultry light, it was looking remarkably like a sepia reproduction of itself. "I think I see Fabia," she said, "and her cicisbeo." Marshall looked at her reproachfully.

Two figures waved briefly at them from a nearby rise, and then began rather carefully to desend it.

"According to this," Marshall held out his guideوook, "we are practically on top of the Golden House."

Alice evinced no interest. "Perhaps it was whisked away in the night," she said.

The driver of the carriage began simultaneously to mutter and to mop his brow. "I fear he's growing impatient," Irving said. "Though I did make a rather generous down payment. What is the Foro Italico, do you suppose?"

"It just rates a couple of lines of fine type in here," Marshall said.

"All I know," Alice said, "is that Abel Greeley puts it right up there with the Victor Emmanuel Monument and the Milan railway station."

"Everything else closed," the driver said. "*Chiuso*, closed."

"They vanished," Mrs. Bridgewater was saying, as a not-too-commodious Simca drew up to the curb.

"Hop in, everybody," Fabia said. "Memmo is taking us to the Protestant Cemetery."

"I am most happy to meet you," Baroness Oscari said. "Especially you," she added, turning toward Dr. Bridgewater. "There have been doctors in my family ever since the Middle Ages."

"It is nice to be in a home again," Mrs. Bridgewater said. She gazed about at the bleak modernity of a room which somehow suggested an upstairs crypt.

"I am only sorry that your son cannot be here," the baroness said. "Fabia has told me so much about him. From her description, he sounds rather like my firstborn, Orazio. He is living in Udine for the time being."

"I understand, Baroness," Dr. Bridgewater said, "that you are a Bryn Mawr girl."

"Yes. The year I spent at Bryn Mawr was—well, if not the happiest, one of the most worthwhile. Have you any connections with Bryn Mawr?"

"No," Dr. Bridgewater said. "None."

"I know for a fact," Mrs. Bridgewater quickly added, "that it is held in very high esteem."

"Please come into the garden now, and meet my husband," the baroness said. "I don't allow him to smoke his cigars in the house."

Dr. Oscari was seated on a stone bench beside a small trickling fountain. He rose to his feet and advanced, smiling shyly. "He doesn't speak English," his wife explained.

Fabia greeted him with an affectionate, *"Buona sera, Dodo."*

"Memmo has been telling me what wonderful tourists you are," the baroness said. "Most Americans, when they come to Rome, want to see only the Forum and the Spanish Steps. You have seen parts of the city that many Romans never see."

Dr. Bridgewater swelled a little. "I find standing here, in Parioli, just as interesting as standing in the Pantheon. The one is the world of today; the other, of yesterday."

Baroness Oscari looked at him with incredulity. After a long pause she said, "Well, there is no accounting for tastes."

Memmo took them on a tour of the garden: the two orange trees, the six oleanders and the vine. At one point something shot across the moist pebbles of the path, causing Mrs. Bridgewater to scream. "Was that an eft?" she asked.

"Why yes," Memmo said, "it was."

Fabia picked a calendula and began to chew the stem. "I'll be sorry to leave this funny old city," she said.

"And how are you progressing with *I Promessi Sposi?*" the baroness asked her.

"Così così," Fabia said. "Though for the life of me I can't see why it reminds Memmo of Proust."

"I understand," Dr. Oscari said to her in Italian, "that you are fond of the work of Raphael Mengs."

"We find we have many tastes in common," Memmo said. "Today it was Canova's sculpture of Pauline Borghese—'La Paolina.'"

"Unfortunately, our stay in Rome will be over all too soon," Dr. Bridgewater said. "We must push on to Naples, and then to Calabria."

"Maybe you will take me along to protect you from bandits," Memmo said. "Bang! Bang!"

His mother frowned. "Calabria is not Sicily," she said. Turning to Mrs. Bridgewater, she continued: "My husband has cousins there, distant cousins. Their lands are vast, but they are not rich." She paused and added, "There is, of course, nothing to eat or drink."

Dr. Oscari flicked his cigar ash into a tub of snapdragons. "Hillbillies," he said in English. He turned to Fabia and spoke to her at some length in Italian. When he had finished, his wife translated succinctly. "He says when she has finished Manzoni, she will be ready for d'Annunzio. It is d'Annunzio who, he considers, has, after Dante, most richly explored the resources of our language. Especially in *La Figlia di Jorio*."

Memmo made a face. "Myself, I prefer Sannazaro."

"While I," the baroness added, "would recommend the novels of Matilde Serao."

Dr. and Mrs. Bridgewater kept their peace.

"How is Mrs. Kelso?" Memmo asked.

"Not too well," Mrs. Bridgewater said with a little cough, indicating that the illness was one which would not bear much discussion.

"I am sorry to hear it," the baroness said. "If there is anything my husband can do—"

"Eno's Fruit Salts," interjected the latter, again in English.

"I think I've found it," Victor said excitedly, as he stuck his head out from under a stripped-down chassis. "It's this doohickey here."

Paul looked at the ominous sky and at a nearby road sign which read, "Aix-les-Bains 71 Km." He said nothing.

Victor got to his feet and gazed about him in growing alarm. Aside from a distant pine, the maquis—if such it was—seemed all that the books had promised. But as his face darkened, Paul's grew bright: over a distant crest appeared something rather like a wood louse. After a considerable time, a Volkswagen approached and stopped on the other side of the road. A pretty seventeen-year-old girl with blonde hair leaned out of the window. "Is this the way to Culoz?" she asked.

"Could be," Victor said. "How about lending us a hairpin so we can fix this darn thing?"

"No," Paul said, "you are well out of your path . . . unless Culoz has moved bag and baggage to the Pyrenees."

"What seems to be the matter with your car?" the girl asked, glancing briefly at her reflection in the rearview mirror.

"We don't use hairpins," her companion said. "You're an American," she said accusingly to Victor.

"We could give you a lift to the nearest garage," the first girl said. "Unless you're going to Culoz. I'm Madge Parkinson, and this is my friend, Dottie Siegel."

After some hopping in and out, and lashing of baggage to the roof, they were hurtling on their way, neck and neck with the gathering storm. "We've done the Loire," Dottie Siegel explained. "Now we're off to a seminar at Salzburg."

"Why are you going to Culoz?" Victor asked.

"Partly to see a brother, but mostly to see the lake about which Lamartine wrote his poem," Madge said. "We're told it's nearby."

"My mother would be interested in that," Victor said. "Anyway I think that's the one."

"I'm not much on poetry," Paul confessed, "but I think the lake you mean is Bourget Lake. Culoz is nowhere near it." His head hit the roof as the car went over a thank-you-ma'am.

"These things get you there," Madge said with a laugh, "but not necessarily in one peice."

Paul rubbed his head acquiescingly. "I think we should stop at a roadside café, if we come to one. These roads can sometimes turn to raging torrents during a storm."

"It's hard to imagine who they would cater to around here," Dottie said.

A small huddled town came into view. When they reached it, all windows were shuttered, and the only sign of life was a cur, which hurled itself against the car with a hideous thud.

"Someone's pet, no doubt," Madge said. She flicked on the radio. A fast-moving accordion polka soon revived their spirits.

Paul sang along for a few bars, then translated. "It tells about a girl—a woman—who waits on the mole for her sailor. When he comes back, first she is going to beat him up, then she is going to show him a good time."

"Well—does she?" Dottie asked.

Paul shrugged. "It is of no importance. The entertainment lies in the low-class argot of her expressions."

A flash of lightning galvanized their attention on a police truck blocking the road ahead. As they approached it, a rubber-clad policeman with a lantern signaled them to stop. He came over to the car.

"The bridge ahead is washed out," he said. "You'll have to turn back, toward Culoz—unless you want to try the Hôtel des Voyageurs, about a quarter of a mile back. It's very comfortable."

Without consulting her companions, Madge made a sharp U-turn. They soon drew up before an inauspicious-looking hostelry. A mustachioed man wearing a blue vest and a beret pulled down over his head came rushing out to take their bags.

"Everyone wants to stay here when it rains," he said amiably. "When the sun shines, everyone passes by." Inside, he set down the bags and made Madge a little bow. "I am the *patron*,

Alfred Duclos. Did you wish double or single beds? I can give you a room with three singles, and another with one double. In the event of a benighted traveler, however, I will have to allow him the third single bed. Perhaps, therefore, the two men would prefer the room with the three beds?"

"Suppose it's a woman," Dottie said.

"Or a couple," Paul added.

"In that case, some other arrangement would be necessary," M. Duclos replied.

A thunderclap rent the air. In the silence that followed, the travelers took in the room in which they stood, its simplicity relieved only by a large photograph of Léon Blum.

M. Duclos gestured toward a row of hoary aperitif bottles on a small stand. "Perhaps," he said, "the ladies would like a Picon . . ." He was cut short by what seemed to be a ball of fire, which roared down the chimney and shot out into the room. The thing vanished as swiftly as it had come, and left behind a strong smell of singed hair. Rain began to fall in torrents and some tiles were heard shattering in the road without.

"It's really too sultry for Picon," Madge said, "but a pastis would be fine."

At the others' request, M. Duclos produced four glasses of Pastis 51, after which he meditatively poured himself a glass of pale yellow Suze. Dottie extracted a box of diet wafers from a wicker hamper and doled out two for Madge and three for herself. "I'm sure *you* will want something more fortifying," she said as she put the box away. And indeed, Paul was soon calling for bread, cheese and anchovies.

Mme. Duclos, a short dark woman of uncertain age, appeared in a doorway. "There is some cold roast lamb," she said, "and I could fix a cheese omelet. For dessert, cheese, and *reines-claudes*."

"What's that?" Madge asked.

"It's like a sour green plum," Paul said.

Mme. Duclos disappeared, and returned with a large Coca-Cola bottle filled with red wine.

Madge said, as she helped herself to a full glass of same, "I couldn't eat another bite."

"How many guests do you have at the moment?" Victor asked, as Mme. Duclos again emerged from the kitchen, this time bearing a cold joint.

Two men came in. Both were dressed in black, soaking wet and cursing loudly and at length. Paul smiled appreciatively. "Here in the south," he explained, "swearing is something of a fine art."

"Those two are college professors from Pau," Mme. Duclos said, as the men were heard tramping upstairs. "We only have two other pensioners—the Misses Tosti, from Paris."

Before Victor could ask the question that leaped to his lips, Claire and Nadia came down the stairs. They were dressed in Austrian walking outfits and singing the "Swing Duet" from *Véronique*. The sight of Victor halted them in mid-trill. Just at that moment, another thunderbolt erupted from the chimney, plunging the hotel in darkness. And there we must leave them for a while.

chapter ten

Mrs. Bridgewater averted her gaze from the flotsam, then looked hastily back, lest she step off the quay and into it. "What I can't get used to," she said, "is the idea of all those Normans way down here." Nearby, some men were chasing a dog, in hopes of hitting it with a paddle.

"Yes, and what about the Greeks?" Mrs. Kelso said. She resumed sucking *granita di limone* from a small paper cup.

"They say that in the interior of the island," Mrs. Bridgewater went on, "one often sees blue-eyed men with red hair: the descendants of the Normans." Her tone was that of someone for whom history has begun to make sense.

"How odd—I didn't know that the Normans had red hair,"

Mrs. Kelso said. "Though I guess I wouldn't recognize one if I tripped over him," she added with a laugh. "Mr. Kelso's grandfather was once the consul here; but I'm afraid he was not well liked. The Scotch was very strong in him. He used to speak bitterly about the bribery, nepotism and general unsanitary conditions. Or so I'm told."

"I've always heard the Sicilians were a very clean people when given a chance," Alice said, with a wink at Memmo.

"They are very short," Memmo said. "It is the Arab blood. Sometimes it makes them sour, moody and passionate."

Mrs. Bridgewater, who disapproved of all three of these qualities, in that order, decided to let the conversation die. It seemed as though they had walked a long distance from their hotel. The late-afternoon shadows had begun to lengthen, but the Conca d'Oro looked no more golden than usual.

"Does anyone have any idea where we are?" Alice pouted. "Maybe those soldiers over there could tell us."

"I know exactly where we are," Mrs. Kelso said.

"Are you Americans?" one of the soldiers asked Alice. "My uncle lives in Cleveland."

"How interesting," Mrs. Kelso said. "I once spent the summer there—well, Shaker Heights. In what part of Cleveland does your uncle live?"

"Euclid Avenue." He turned to Alice. "What state are you from?"

"You know, Di," Mrs. Kelso said in an undertone, "Euclid Avenue is the longest street in the world."

"New York," Alice said. "The state—not the city."

"When I finish my military service," the soldier said, "I will go to America and work in my uncle's restaurant. Not my uncle in Cleveland, my uncle in New York."

"What does your uncle in Cleveland do?" Alice asked.

"He has a restaurant: the Luna Gardens. It is very well known."

"Is this lady your sister?" another soldier asked, jerking his thumb in the direction of Fabia.

"No," Mrs. Bridgewater said. "This is my daughter. We also have another child, a boy, though he is quite grown now. He is in France."

"You are French?" the second soldier asked.

"Ah, *la Francia*," the first soldier smiled. He chuckled. "My name is Giorgio Grossblatt. From Trento. This is my friend Epifanio—Epifanio Montemezzi."

"From Pozzuoli."

"Isn't Sophia Loren from Pozzuoli?" Fabia asked.

"You bet," Epifanio said. "We are all crazy about her." He winked at Memmo, who was standing somewhat apart.

The third soldier, who had been looking a bit suspiciously at the Americans, now joined the group. "What kind of car do you drive?" he asked Mrs. Kelso.

"A Studebaker—though for years we always had a Dodge."

"What time did you say you made the reservations for, Memmo?" Mrs. Bridgewater asked.

"Ten-thirty," Fabia intervened. "The whole point is to eat in the garden, but the guidebook says you aren't safe from the bugs until after dark."

"What restaurant is that?" the third soldier asked.

"The Villa Igiea," Memmo said. "Have you been there?"

"Often," was the reply.

"Would you say that it is the best restaurant in Palermo?" Mrs. Bridgewater asked.

"The best, no. The most expensive, yes."

"Roberto is a millionaire," Epifanio explained to Mrs. Bridgewater in a kindly way.

"Which would you say *is* the best restaurant here?" Mrs. Kelso asked.

"There is none," Roberto said.

Mrs. Bridgewater's uneasiness crystallized in a manner not

unfamiliar to her family. "Would you care to join us for an aperitif?" she asked.

Despite the vagaries of Mrs. Kelso's bump of locality, they were soon seated at a sidewalk table on the Via Cavour.

"It's just like Ives' Fourth," Alice said to Fabia, but her remark was lost in the din.

"If your stomach is feeling uneasy," Roberto said to Alice, with a sudden air of *savoir-faire*, "I recommend the Rabarbaro Zucca. It's made of rhubarb, and tastes like medicine."

"No thanks," Alice said. "I don't want anything stronger than a Bellini. Though you tempt me strangely."

A flurry among the further tables caused many to rise to their feet. After a while, a donkey, festooned with feathers and pulling a gaily painted cart, trotted by.

"*Giorno di festa*," explained Giorgio. "A holiday."

"Which one?" Mrs. Kelso asked.

"Not an important one," Roberto said. "In Italy, anything that is thought nice is called *giorno di festa*." He sent a penetrating look in the direction of the nearest waiter, who said, "*Subito*," and vanished. Roberto turned back to Fabia. "Now I must ask you something. What do you think of the Italian men?"

Alice snorted and began to wave. A waiter came and took their order.

"Actually I haven't met enough of them to know," Fabia said with a studied grace. "However, the ones I have met, I've liked."

"In America," Mrs. Kelso said in an unmistakable tone, "the problems of the *mezzogiorno* are a cause of grave concern." She apparently expected a comment from Roberto, but none was forthcoming, though their drinks were.

Alice sipped her Rabarbaro Zucca and began to choke violently. The others stared at her anxiously. When she had caught her breath and wiped her eyes, they did not—as some had anticipated—reap the whirlwind.

"Needs must when the devil drives," Alice said, and ordered another with a glass of San Pellegrino on the side.

Mrs. Bridgewater, who was gazing about her, suddenly gave a start. "Fabia!" she said. "That boy over there—the one in shorts—doesn't he look just like Victor?"

"Since the woman on his arm is Nadia Tosti," Fabia said, "I don't find the resemblance all that surprising."

"Shall we ask them to join us?" Memmo said, in a bewildered but willing tone.

Before they do so, however, let us move back several weeks in time, and a good many kilometers to the north, to the Hôtel des Voyageurs.

After an acetylene lamp was brought and the surprise and the introductions were over, a bottle of local wine was broached (the *patron* having silently removed the Coca-Cola bottle on Claire's appearing). A small silence fell—or as much of one as the weather permitted.

Madge was the first to break it. "That was very pretty— what you were singing," she said. "I wish you'd sing it all the way through, from beginning to end."

"Only this time I will take the man's part," Paul said, "and 'push.' "

This bit of innuendo caused Claire to say, "Your mother and the doctor, Victor: how do they sustain the fatigues of travel?"

Victor pondered this question for some moments before replying. "I guess it's traveling with friends," he said. "it's not so tiring when other people around you are tired."

"It must be wonderful to travel in France *and* be French," Dottie said. "I'm constantly torn between some cathedral and something a little more recherché."

"Yes, we often find little out-of-the way places," Nadia said with a good-natured laugh, "such as this."

Claire winced as some more tiles came clattering down into the courtyard outside. "But *you*—how did you ever find it?"

When Paul had told them, not without exaggeration and some Gallic gestures, his face settled into a worried frown. "Boy, that car—I don't know what's going to happen."

"Don't worry," said one of the two teachers from Pau, who had returned to the bar and had for some time been trying unsuccessfully to join in the conversation. "These country roads can turn into torrents overnight. Your car is probably at the bottom of the Rhone River by now."

"Yes," Madge said, "once again it's the Volkswagen *über alles*." She drained her glass and, turning to Victor, said, "Would you do the honors?"

"*Mais certainement*," replied Victor, whose cheeks were beginning to glow. "Another bottle of your *pinard*, Monsieur Duclos, *s'il vous plaît*—'with beaded bubbles winking at the brim.'"

"That's Keats, isn't it," the other teacher said. "I didn't know Americans read Keats. I'm very fond of Dashiell Hammett," he added quickly. Finding his overtures were not rebuffed, he continued. "I am Etienne Gilot, and this is my colleague, Marc Ducasse."

"Any relation to Isidor—the second most famous *Palois* of them all?" Victor asked, with the air of one who has the ball and is running with it. Nadia gasped in admiration.

"I am reminded," Claire said, "of that villa outside Florence, the one Boccaccio made the scene of his *Decameron*. Though in this instance, it is the rain that plagues us."

"That gives me an idea," Etienne said. "Why don't we try to stave off boredom by telling each other stories? But I warn you, I know a few racy ones."

"I," Nadia said, "am not unreminded of 'The Masque of the Red Death.'"

M. Duclos returned and raised his eyes despairingly to the ceiling. "I couldn't find you any wine—the cellar's flooded. But I've brought you a bottle of my homemade *digestif*."

He poured a small amount into a glass and offered it to Marc Ducasse, who accepted it warily. When he had sipped it, rolled it in his mouth and swallowed it, he said, "My good man, you have here cause for future fame and fortune."

Mme. Duclos nodded knowingly. "He could have sold the formula ten times over," she said. "The Fernet-Branca people have been pestering him for it for years. But he likes to keep it for himself and a few cronies."

Claire gazed questioningly at the inky liquid in her glass. "What is its base?" she asked.

"Galoshes, I *think*," Dottie murmured. This aside was not lost on M. Duclos, who looked at her in an injured manner but said nothing.

The door opened to admit a figure in streaming black rubber. The room was briefly but thoroughly lashed by the tempest. "The road has become a torrent," the new arrival announced.

"Good evening, *Monsieur l'Agent*," the proprietress said officiously. "What can I get you? A little glass of *digestif*, perhaps?"

"No, I have to work," was the glum reply.

"You have been wondering how it is that you find us here," Claire said to Victor. She spoke as one who has glanced into *Robert's Rules of Order* and now takes up the gavel.

"No I haven't," Victor said.

Claire smiled at him benignly and went on. "My sister Nadia is nearing the end of a long search. One of her clients—a wealthy American who, as you say, prefers to remain anonymous—has for a long time sought to locate a missing work—a sculpture of Hiram Powers. We have good reason to think that right now it is gathering dust somewhere in the environs of Culoz."

The gendarme eyed her narrowly. "What does this statue represent?" he asked.

"The goddess Demeter, with her daughter Proserpine kneeling before her and holding a sheaf of bachelor buttons in her outstretched arms."

The policeman nodded. "I think I know that work," he said. "It stands in the Cours Lamartine, at Annemasse. There has been a campaign in the press lately to have it removed."

"You have been most helpful," Nadia said. When the policeman turned to speak with the *patron*, she said in a lower voice, "I am well acquainted with the work of which he speaks. It represents the people of the Ile Bourbon—as it was then called—offering tribute to the mother country—or some such. It is by a minor follower of Barye and is of no interest whatsoever. Not even a sledgehammer could reduce it to viable fragments."

"Well, you have to give him A for Effort," Victor said. "But seriously, Nadia, do you have any idea where the statue really is?"

The policeman, after downing (on second thought) a large glass of rum at the bar, returned to their table. "My good friends," he said, pressing his fingertips together, "you must be prepared to evacuate this place, should it become necessary. The whole mountain might land on us at any moment."

As he stopped speaking, Madge was heard murmuring to Paul, "Would you mind pouring me another glass of that moustache straightener?"

Victor admired Nadia for wanting to go to Annemasse anyway, to "check out the statue," as she put it. Late the following day, having survived the perils of the Hôtel des

Voyageurs, a group of four young people was seen alighting from a mud-spattered Peugeot in the Cours Lamartine. The storm of the previous day had broken summer's back, and some chill air was leaking down from the none-too-distant mountains. A dank smell arose from the ground and the pollarded catalpas seemed to gesticulate vehemently in the twilight.

Claire glanced skeptically at the stubby trunks. "You will recall," she said, "how Stendhal inveighed against such treatment of trees. He seemed to think it exclusively a French vice—but then, he, too, suffered from *l'anglomanie.*"

"As a film," Paul said, "I prefer *The Charterhouse.*"

They stopped before a statue that seemed to represent a giant pineapple over whose surface tiny figures climbed. "You see? I was right," Nadia said despairingly.

"It seems to have been carved out of marl," Paul suggested.

"We can't give up this easily," Victor said, with grim determination. Taking Nadia's arm, he hustled them further along the Cours. They soon came to yet another statue: the poet Lamartine himself, surrounded by the creatures of his imagination. His favorite of these seemed to be an impish peasant girl, whom the Tosti sisters identified as Graziella.

"The flowers are nice," Victor said, indicating the wheel of yellow cannas from which the monument rose. As they were returning to the car, Victor vanished toward a *châlet de nécessité* that sat in a nearby clump of rhododendrons. He reappeared almost immediately, too excited for speech but gasping and pointing in the direction whence he came. Without a word, he turned and retraced his steps, the others following in silent haste. There, within the clump and turned toward the wall, was an unmistakable, if somewhat weather-stained, Hiram Powers.

For once, even Claire lost her cool. "Good grief!" she exclaimed.

Victor was radiant, and Nadia seemed not unwilling to divide her attention between the object of her long hunt and its finder. However, she contented herself with saying, "This must be looked into."

The following day—after a visit to the *Syndicat d'Initiative*—she rejoined the others, who, having returned to the scene of their triumph, were seated around a table outside a little thatched bungalow in the Cours Lamartine. All hung upon her words, of which, to make a long story short, the burden was as follows.

For many years Demeter and her daughter had stood in the entrance hall of a Gothicized chateau outside the town, which, passing through various hands, eventually came into those of an austere maiden lady. The maiden, or rather, the lady, finding so many and such evident breasts unworthy of the kinship she claimed to General Boulanger, had offered it forthwith to the town fathers on extended loan. She, her kin—even the chateau—had passed from the scene long since, and the present town fathers were only too anxious to disembarrass themselves of a work that gave rise to many a schoolboy ribaldry. The campaign for its removal, initiated by the local Communist paper, soon gained numerous adherents of every political stripe, and had successfully progressed as far as the rhododendrons, when the town was riven by the question of what work was to replace it. At the moment, the leading contenders were a concrete dove, symbolizing peace, and an abstraction of St. Francis de Sales. And it was further rumored that in far-off Paris a thunderbolt was being readied.

"In other words," Nadia said, "the Hirman Powers is up for grabs."

How the controversial work of art was finally removed from Annemasse under cover of night, and, after many difficulties, crated and shipped to the United States, need not concern our readers. Suffice it to say that it eventually found its way to a grape arbor on a Long Island estate where it stands to this day.

The next morning, after a night spent mastering the fundamentals of the maxixe, Victor was at the wheel of the Peugeot with Nadia seated beside him, as the little band set out for Geneva and the Place du Molard. Claire had suggested a visit to Ferney, and in a flash the others agreed. But as luck would have it, a telegram was waiting for Paul at the hotel, summoning him a week early to Monza. And so, after a hasty fondue and a stroll past the house where Calvin had lived, they again sped on their way, slowing up a bit only at Chillon.

Perhaps it was the local white wine, perhaps it was the nuptial connotations of the Alps, but Victor and Nadia abruptly found themselves living in a state of what Victor called "sin." Let it be quickly added in his defense that he thought of this condition as a necessary prelude to the altar, nor did the French girl require much cajoling.

"What isn't clear to me," Mrs. Bridgewater said, "is who this Madge and Dottie are, and where they figure in it."

"Yes," Dr. Bridgewater agreed, "that is one of the things that's none too clear."

Victor smiled patiently. "I told you before, they picked us up in the south of France. Just before a storm. They probably saved our lives," he mused.

Dr. Bridgewater's face assumed an expression usually reserved for the AMA. "I wonder if you are aware of what it costs—in money—to maintain a family these days? Take an apartment in New York for example, quite a small apartment . . ."

"I was coming to that," Victor said. "Nadia isn't sure she'd feel happy living in America. In fact, she'd rather live in Paris."

Mrs. Bridgewater drifted over to the window, and stood

gazing at the sunlit Mediterranean. Reacting to this as though it were his cue, Dr. Bridgewater asked in sepulchral tones, "And what would you do in Paris?"

"I was coming to that," Victor chuckled. "Nadia has a friend who works on the desk at the *Herald Tribune* there. She thinks he could get me a job rewriting, at least until I learn the antique business."

The incredulity with which this was received caused Victor to continue. "Anyway, that's not our long-range plan."

"What is your long-range plan, dear?" Mrs. Bridgewater encouraged.

Victor frowned as he marshaled his thoughts. "Well," he said. "Europeans are crazy about American antiques. Claire is fed up with the perfume game, but she doesn't like to give up the travel. So the scheme is this. We open an American antique shop in Paris. Claire does the buying."

"I have heard of bringing coals to Newcastle," Dr. Bridgewater said, "but this takes the cake."

Mrs. Bridgewater suddenly wheeled around and smiled at them coquettishly. "Well, Father," she said, "you know we always said we wouldn't stand in their way when the time came, and I guess it has. Besides, she must be a pretty smart girl if that story about the Hiram Powers is true."

A brief rat-a-tat at the door preceded the entrance of a cheerful Fabia. She was dressed in various shades of lemon and sported an enormous pair of sunglasses. "Is Victor still on the coals?" she asked. "Or can he be taken off long enough so we won't miss the trip to Cefalù?"

"There are times, Fabia," Dr. Bridgewater said, "when I wonder where my children got their sense of humor. Certainly not from your mother or me."

Fabia pouted. "Are you including Victor in that? Mrs. Kelso doesn't seem to think I'm so bad. She just called me her sunshine girl."

122

Mrs. Bridgewater sighed. "Mildred just says the first thing that pops into her head."

"Oh I don't mind that," Fabia said. "It's one of her nicer qualities. But I didn't come here to discuss Mrs. Kelso, I came to get the lowdown on Victor. Are he and Nadia getting spliced, or are they not?"

"That's about the size of it," Victor said.

His father began to heave in his chair, but Mrs. Bridgewater intervened. "It's nothing that won't keep," she said. "I thought Alice would be with you."

Fabia shrugged. "I guess she's wandered off in the direction of the barracks again."

"Oh," Mrs. Bridgewater said quietly. "I hope she won't do anything rash."

"Alice never does anything rash. She just gives that impression," Victor said with his newfound assurance. "Anyway, she's gone to Monreale with Nadia. There's an old man up there who makes some kind of special straw hats to order. I'm sure glad they hit it off so well." His tone was one of simple relief.

"To wear?" Fabia asked. "Or to stuff a boutique with?"

"Aw, can it, Sis," Victor scowled.

Fabia continued to parade up and down in the tiny *salotto*. "I never thought I'd have Claire Tosti for an in-law," she said. "I guess there are worse things, though offhand I can't think of any."

"I wouldn't tempt fate if I were you," Victor said, in a surprisingly malicious tone.

"You're already getting to be quite French, aren't you," Fabia said.

"Now, children," Mrs. Bridgewater said. She began dabbing at her cheeks with a small lace handkerchief. At that moment the door opened and Memmo entered, resplendent in a pale pongee suit. "All aboard!" he called. "The Cefalù choochoo is leaving on track twenty-nine."

Mrs. Bridgewater surveyed her hankie. "Is this large enough, Fabia? To drop on my head, for the churches?"

"All that is asked," Dr. Bridgewater said, "is a gesture. Well, are we waiting for Mildred Kelso?"

Memmo laughed. "Not at all," he said. "She is already in the car, and not unmindful of the passing time."

"I don't know quite what I expected of Favorita," Alice said, "but it certainly wasn't palm trees and yuccas."

"Me too," Fabia chimed in, after yawning. "I guess I was expecting—well, something like nineteenth-century Paris. The gaslit era."

"It is true," Giorgio Grossblatt said. "Sicily is not cozy—it is not *gemütlich*. In fact, Italy is not *gemütlich*. Except in the Trento area, and some other parts of the north."

"I'm glad Italy isn't *gemütlich*," Alice said. "I don't think I could stand it if it was."

Ever since lunch, Roberto had appeared plunged in a stupor. He now came to long enough to say, "Sicily is a hostile land. It is also a garden."

"And a dump," Giorgio said.

"Oh, it's OK," Alice said, glancing about at the arid hills through which they sped. "Say—isn't it too bad about Memmo getting that urgent call back to Rome. I mean, he was the one who *wanted* to go to Segesta."

Fabia looked mysterious and restive.

"Segesta!" Roberto said. "No self-respecting Italian would dare miss it—it is Sicily's Leaning Tower of Pisa. In fact, why don't we make a detour, a kind of *viaggio sorprèsa?* It is the hill towns that are most typically characteristic."

The girls glanced apprehensively toward the heights, and Alice said, "I don't feel up to a tussle with Salvatore Giuliano this afternoon. Anyway, we have to be back at five—Fabia's expecting a phone call."

"From Rome?" Roberto asked. "We could not possibly get back from Segesta by five." He turned onto a secondary road which sloped steeply upward, where they soon encountered a herd of goats.

"The owner is swearing at me," Roberto said as he plowed through the flock, causing a certain amount of caprine hysteria, "but I can't understand him. He's speaking in Sicilian dialect."

Their merriment, if such it was, abruptly ceased. Beyond the next curve the road wound on in a series of dramatic S's, skirting what appeared to be The Abyss.

"Well," Giorgio said, "we can't go back—and I certainly hate like hell to go on."

But Roberto had already recovered his aplomb. "Don't worry," he said. "I am a professional racing-car driver. I have driven in the *Mille Miglie,* and at Monza." With that, he stepped on the accelerator and sent the car hurtling forward in a manner reminiscent of the late Barney Oldfield.

A couple of thrilling kilometers later, they came within sight of some hovels, partly surrounded by a dilapidated wall. Roberto slowed down. The engine gave a brief summary of Elektra's dance of triumph and, like Elektra, died.

A deep silence ensued. Fabia glanced nervously at the nearest hovel, whose facade bore the tattered remnants of an advertisement for Pirelli tires. "Do you suppose that's a garage?" she asked Roberto in a half-whisper.

"Possibly," he said. But he showed no inclination to get out and investigate. Meanwhile the distant, faintly vengeful bleating of goats became audible.

"I think someone should go knock on that door," Alice said. Before anyone could do so it opened of its own accord and a very old lady dressed in black emerged. At the sight of our friends, she threw up her hands in dismay and withdrew into the house, slamming and locking the door behind her.

After a reproachful silence, Giorgio said, "I guess this will take some looking into." He gave a little cough and added, "Don't you think so, Roberto?"

"And the sooner the better," Alice said.

A military truck, bristling with what Alice was later to describe as state troopers, approached the stranded vehicle and ground to a halt. The driver peered curiously at Roberto. "It's against the law to stop here," he said. There followed ten minutes of loud and lively give-and-take, at the end of which the driver of the truck descended, opened the hood of Roberto's car and set whatever was wrong to rights—a service for which he seemed to feel amply repaid by a pack of Fabia's Philip Morris. Again Roberto pressed the accelerator and the Lancia jolted forward, leaving the enthusiastically waving *carabinieri* and a cloud of dust in its wake.

Roberto, who was sulky, drove even faster than before, and they were soon whizzing through some artichoke plantations. Fabia gave a little scream as they came over a rise and saw, far below them, the temple at Segesta. It stood, or rather lay from their point of view, on a gray-green patch, much as Goethe had found it and Augustus Hare had left it—except for the buses, by which it was almost entirely surrounded.

Dusk has long since set in by the time they drew up before the Albergo delle Palme. Fabia quickly paid Roberto such skimpy *devoirs* as she felt were due and went inside, but it took Alice and Giorgio somewhat longer to become disentangled.

chapter eleven

Martha opened the Bridgewaters' front door and showed Marshall into the living room. A pleasant scene met his eyes. Mrs. Bridgewater was seated before the fireplace, in which a cheerful fire was burning, bent upon her embroidery frame where an intricate floral design involving parrot tulips had begun to take shape. Nearby, Fabia was ensconced in a "Sleepy Hollow" chair, dozing over a recent number of *Yale French Studies*. At the far end of the room Dr. Bridgewater was accompanying his own rich bass-baritone at the spinet in a swinging rendition of "The Lowland Sea."

"Here's Mr. Bush," Martha said. She waited until Marshall

was about to speak, then went on: "I still haven't gotten to the bottom of those gem pans," and left.

Balthazar, the Bridgewaters' aged Chesapeake Bay retriever, came bounding into the room and jumped up against Marshall, almost knocking him off balance. Marshall was one of his favorites.

After he had cuffed the dog and given his ears a few hard yanks, Marshall again began to speak. This time Mrs. Bridgewater forestalled him. "That dog is simply crazy about you."

"Yes," he said, "I see."

Dr. Bridgewater, whose song had died away like distant thunder, spoke in a welcoming though somewhat impatient voice. "Come in and sit down, Marshall; come in and sit down. What news of Alice—of 'Sweet Alice, Ben Bolt'? How did that go, Mother?"

Fabia's upper lip curled slightly. "Have you come to tell us that the grand opening of the Ristorante Trentino is slated for the foreseeable future?" she asked.

"No, I haven't," Marshall said. His attention was given to choosing between a distant, but comfortable, Chesterfield and a Windsor chair which he well knew had more than the usual number of spindles in its back. Finally he eased himself cautiously into the latter. "I've come to ask for your set of keys to our house, and to ask you to a spaghetti dinner Alice is throwing in honor of our guest."

"Lasagne is what Alice told me," Fabia said. "They're making it from scratch."

"From scratch?" Mrs. Bridgewater wondered.

"Yes, the dough is draped over most of the kitchen chairs at the moment—another reason for this visit," Marshall said.

"Your little house must be bursting at the seams." Dr. Bridgewater smiled appreciatively. "Now, about the keys. Fabia, if you would be so good, in my desk, in the study . . ."

"Actually," Fabia said, "they're upstairs in my bag. I nipped over the other day to retrieve my copy of *Piccolo Mondo Antico*."

Marshall seemed to ponder this, but said nothing. Oddly enough, neither did her parents.

"Oh, for Pete's sake," Fabia said, "Alice said she'd finished with it."

"I do envy Alice," Mrs. Bridgewater said. "Our vegetable man tells me she's made amazing progress in Italian. She can do anything she wants to, once she sets her mind to it."

Balthazar had been sitting on the hearthrug, staring dopily into the fire. Now he lifted his head and gave a long, spine-chilling howl. The others in the room seemed stunned.

"Mercy—he never did that before," Mrs. Bridgewater said.

"Doesn't it mean someone is going to die?" Fabia said. "Or has already?"

"Let's hope it's someone in *his* family," Marshall said.

For some reason this remark precipitated another explosion of friendliness in Balthazar, who lunged at Marshall and began plastering him with kisses. When Mrs. Bridgewater had succeeded in coaxing him back to the hearthrug, she asked Marshall, "And how is Giorgio adjusting to life over here?"

"I don't suppose he ever will," Marshall said, "at least, not as long as Alice persists in speaking nothing but Italian. The other evening we went for a drive to show him the Walt Whitman Shopping Plaza. They both started jabbering a mile a minute in J. C. Penney's. I walked out and left them there."

"Oh, Marshall." Mrs. Bridgewater smiled at him disapprovingly.

"When is the restaurant going to open?" Fabia asked.

"How would I know?" Marshall said. "I don't speak Italian."

"Mr. Calandro—that's the vegetable man's name—says it will be very soon," Mrs. Bridgewater said. "Alice and Giorgio took him over to see it one day. He says the inside will be beautiful when it's finished."

"Which reminds me, Marshall," Fabia said. "How did you like the stockfish Trento style the other evening?"

Marshall looked at her blankly. "Oh, I like everything he cooks . . ."

For some minutes Dr. Bridgewater had appeared plunged in meditation. Now he removed his pipe from his lips and spoke. "It has been a revivifying experience for Alice. We were commenting on it the other night at supper and saying that she really has come out of her shell."

Martha entered in silent Space Shoes. "It's all right," she said, "after all."

"Why thank you, Martha," Mrs. Bridgewater said to her retreating figure. To the others she added, "Where else would gem pans be, if not in the kitchen?"

"What about Victor?" Marshall asked Dr. Bridgewater. "Has he found work in Paris yet?"

Dr. Bridgewater got to his feet. "Such news," he said as he left the room, "I would scarcely keep under a bushel."

"I didn't mean to offend him," Marshall said.

"Oh it's all right," Fabia said. "A little trip to his humidor is just a form of punctuation."

The electric chime in the hall pealed. "Oh oh," Fabia said, "I have a feeling I know who that is. *Piccolo Mondo Antico* indeed." Nor was she wrong.

"*Ciao ciao ciao!*" Alice said as she headed for the fire with outstretched hands. "*Com' è bello! Come mi piace—che fuoco!*"

"Alice," Fabia said, "you've got to be kidding."

Ignoring this sally, Alice gazed about the room as though it were unfamiliar. Giorgio, for whom it must have been more of a novelty, paid it no mind as he breezed in. After shaking hands with the ladies he joined Alice and Balthazar on the hearthrug.

Because of his accent (not reproduced here), Mrs. Bridgewater had formed the habit of speaking to him as though he were a child. "Good evening, Giorgio," she said rather loudly. "Have you heard from your home? How is your mother? And your sisters, how are they?" She was going to ask about the latter in more detail, but did not, recollecting that their number was eleven.

"Oh, fair," was the reply.

A peculiar wet noise was heard approaching. Balthazar ran to greet it. "Ah," Dr. Bridgewater said, as he continued to draw on his pipe, "Ah," He nodded and looked about him. Alice gave place, and he began to scrape the dottle from his pipe into the fire.

"We've just come from the ristorante," Alice explained. "Giorgio's been antiquing the beams all afternoon. Unfortunately, they sent us the wrong kind of Tennessee pitch pine."

"I thought it was going to be more of a trattoria than a restaurant," Fabia said.

"No," Giorgio said. "No ristorante and no trattoria. More like a locanda—an osteria, if you prefer."

Huge slow puffs of snow-apple pipe tobacco smoke began to roll through the room. Dr. Bridgewater had, once more, triumphed over his briar.

"It will be both Italian and Tyrolean," Giorgio continued. "That way we hope to attract both the German food lovers and the Italian."

Alice glanced idly at a postcard on the mantelpiece which showed artists sketching in the Place du Tertre. "What's with Victor?" she asked.

Fabia was saying, "If you can tell from the message on that . . ." when Martha ushered in yet another caller: Abel Greeley.

"If it's Victor you want to know about," Abel said, "I'm your man." And indeed, over the summer he had shot up like the proverbial beanstalk. His sideburns were long and he was nattily dressed in a turtleneck sweater, tight-fitting trousers and a suede bush jacket.

"Really," Alice drawled. "And how would you know?"

"Because he wrote me," Abel said, joining the others on the already crowded hearthrug and hooking his heels over the fender. "You see, he'd promised to send me some Louise Brooks stills from the Cinémathèque and I wrote him asking where they were. It seems he and Nadia were married in a civil ceremony at the *Mairie du Seizième*. Her parents are livid—*they* were planning a full-blown church thing, besides which Victor is American. They took off briefly to the Dalmatian coast, and now they're back in Paris. Victor is working as Nadia's assistant in the shop. They'll both be coming here soon, though, because the millionaire that Nadia got the Powers for has commissioned her to do the decorations for his daughter's coming-out party."

Fabia, anticipating tears and a staggering exit from the room, went swiftly to her mother's side. It was the doctor, however, who was in need—though of what, apparently only his wife knew.

"Well, Sam," she said, "Auntie always meant the children to have the principle, so I didn't see why Victor shouldn't have the interest now. His share, of course."

With an aplomb that matched his outfit, Abel chose this moment to say, "Hi, Alice. Hi, Giorgio." Turning to the still nonplussed Bridgewaters, he continued on a more serious note. "Anyway, I gather that Nadia herself has Great Expectations. Her father makes all the lead paint for the battleships of France. Seems he's already taken a certain shine to Victor, and if they'll just consent to go through it again in a church, all will be forgiven."

Mrs. Bridgewater, who a few moments ago had held the threads of life in a steady hand, reverted. "Oh dear," she said, "I hope Victor won't become enmeshed in the material side of things." Like the Lady of Shalott, she rose up from her embroidery frame. "I never dreamed of a military connection!"

"I wouldn't worry, Mrs. Bridgewater," Abel said. "There's something awfully *opéra bouffe* about the French navy."

"It was my understanding," Fabia said, as she wandered off toward the angel-wing begonia, "that they don't use all *that* much lead paint in the French navy nowadays. On the other hand, I guess nobody's about to starve."

Giorgio, who had been feeling at a loss, finally said, "I think this calls for a good stiff drink—to toast the happy pair, I mean."

Dr. Bridgewater shot him a jaundiced look as his wife summoned Martha and commanded, "Champagne."

The guests had scarcely had time to comment variously on the popping of the cork and the excellence of the vintage when the front door opened and Mrs. Greeley, vivacious in a new squirrel coat, rushed in.

"*Scusi,*" she said, "but Abel made me promise to rescue him from all you lovely people when the time came. Alan Watts is giving a talk on the macrobiotic diet at the high school."

Abel drained his glass and turned on his mother a glance with which Don Juan might have greeted the Commendatore. After abbreviated farewells the two disappeared into the gathering dusk.

"It's certainly not the same around here without Fabia," Betty Burgoyne said cheerfully.

"You said that last week," Marshall grumbled. "Or maybe it was last month." He did not look up from the L. L. Bean catalogue through which he was slowly making his way.

Betty sighed in a way that somehow indicated pity for Marshall rather than chagrin at the rebuke. "If no one ever repeated themselves, precious little work would get done," she suggested lightly.

"Work doesn't get done," a new voice said, "one abandons it." This version of Valéry's dictum was spoken by Fabia, who had just entered the office arm in arm with Alice.

"Why, we were just talking about you," Betty gasped.

"Yes," Marshall said, closing the catalogue after a lingering look at a suit of thermal underwear. "She was saying the place isn't the same without you. I only wish I could agree."

"Fabia," Betty exclaimed, "that coat is *so* deceptively simple!"

Alice, on the other hand, had preferred a suit of "blanket plaid," from Old England, on the Boulevard des Capucines, as she later explained to a dubious but dissimulating Betty.

"To what do we owe the honor of this visit?" Marshall asked.

Fabia seated herself in the one conference chair his office allowed and undid her coat, disclosing further simplicities. "Must there be a reason?" she said.

"Since you ask," Alice said, "we've come to take Irving and Mildred to lunch at Giorgio's uncle's restaurant. You know, we've never had them over," she added, accusingly. "Asdrubale—Giorgio's uncle—wants to meet all his friends. Of course you don't have to come."

Marshall had one of his rare flights of affability. "Oh, I don't know. How's the eggplant parmigiana?"

"Delicious," Alice said. "By the way, it's on Grand Street, near the Bowery. We'll have to take a taxi."

It suddenly occurred to Marshall that a change had taken place in Alice. Her former aggressive reserve had been replaced by something else, but he could not tell what. "Where Grand Street meets the Bowery—it's not all that handy," he hedged.

"Your first appointment isn't until three-thirty," Betty offered.

"You could always meet us there if you change your mind,"

Alice said. She got up and made a leisurely tour of the office, pausing at a photograph of a pristine factory beneath a sky of gentian blue.

"Oh come on, Marshall," Fabia snapped, "don't be such a killjoy. I gather the old man is planning some kind of big blowout. He's very anxious to meet Alice's family and, as you well know, you're it."

"Much as I would enjoy clocking Mrs. Kelso's reactions to the Bowery . . ." Marshall was beginning, when he was interrupted by the entrance of the lady and her son.

"Hail hail the gang's all here," said the latter, while the former supplied the counterpoint for a change: "Alice—Fabia —Miss Burgoyne—Marshall."

"And Cottontail," Alice murmured.

After a considerable time, the group—Betty had joined them at Fabia's insistence—found itself reassembled around a sextet of martinis in the spacious back room of the Golfo Azzuro. Giorgio, who had been learning the restaurant business from his uncle since arriving in the States, gestured happily at them from time to time through the plate-glass wall that separated the dining room from the kitchen.

"How clean everything looks," Mrs. Kelso said.

"Spotless," Betty agreed.

Uncle Asdrubale, who was hovering and beaming over them, wagged his chin. "It is clean—not like Italy, huh? New York is a clean city no matter what people say." Mrs. Kelso looked alarmed. "In here," he added.

Marshall drained his martini to the lees, and it was hastily replenished by a waiter of Michelangelesque appearance.

"Best damn martini in New York," their host said. The waiter, all flashing eyes and teeth, rushed off with the pitcher. "Dumb like an ox," Asdrubale divulged.

"What's his name?" Fabia asked.

"Memmo," was the reply. "Memmo da Calabria."

"Is that his last name?"

"No. He is from there. It is a place in southern Italy." His manner changed. "And now, to begin with, the fruit of the sea soup. Just like bouillabaisse only better."

"To begin with . . .?" Mildred Kelso asked faintly.

Memmo reappeared with a steaming tureen whose interior revealed a bewildering array of denizens of the deep. "Try one of the sea dates," Asdrubale said, helping her to a lobed monster.

Fabia smiled at the waiter and spoke to him in Italian.

"What was that?" Marshall asked. Something slithered off his spoon and back into the plate.

"She said, 'Heavy on the mussels,'" Uncle Asdrubale explained.

"Not even in the wilds of Lucania," Marshall muttered.

Giorgio materialized in the dining room, his brow streaming with sweat and a beatific expression on his face. He suggested a figure in Murillo's "The Angels' Kitchen." "How is the soup?" he asked. "Spicy enough?" Without waiting for a reply he extended a hand and said, "You must be Mrs. Kelso's little boy Irving."

"Indeed I am," Irving said, struggling awkwardly to his feet and upsetting his martini glass in the process. ("Memmo—the talcum powder—quick!" Asdrubale thundered.) "Delighted, I'm sure. I've heard a lot about you."

"You bet." Giorgio spread his hands and held them above the fuming tureen. "Today I minced parsley with a cleaver. Look: no Band Aids."

At the mention of Band Aids, Mrs. Kelso's face grew wistful. "If only Fluffy were here to enjoy all this." She withdrew a handkerchief from the crocodile bag Irving had brought her from Florida and blew her nose. That done, she briskly returned to her accustomed brass tacks. "Well, dear, aren't we to be treated to a little announcement on this festive occasion?" She leered at Alice.

"Possibly, but I don't think it's up to me to make it," Alice said, turning to inspect a semiallegorical mural of the Island of Elba and its history.

Memmo returned with the talcum and began shaking it vigorously onto Irving's lap. As the latter wheezed and choked his protests, the powder began to settle on the food.

"*Scemo!*" Uncle Asdrubale roared and frog-marched him from the room.

Under cover of the uproar, Fabia whispered to Mrs. Kelso, "Actually, I don't think Alice has planned any announcement—for today."

"Then why are we here?" Mrs. Kelso asked.

Giorgio frowned at the unwonted garniture on the fruit of the sea soup. "That guy is so dumb he makes me sick," he said. "Wait—I'll bring you new bowls and a new bowl of soup."

"Why don't we just skip ahead to the rollatine?" Alice said. Her voice betrayed a certain strain. "Marshall, since you are the nearest thing to a father I have, would you make the announcement?"

A bottle of Est Est Est was produced and Marshall, in a speech, informed their startled friends that Alice and Giorgio were married, and had been since the mayor of Palermo pronounced the few necessary words.

Fabia's jaw dropped. "You mean that morning you were supposed to go to Monreale . . . ?

"Yes," Alice replied smugly. "Nadia and Roberto were the witnesses. Afterward we had a fish lunch on the wharves. While *you* were all at Cefalù."

"I too was a runaway bride," Mrs. Kelso said, while Betty wailed, "If only my mother could be here!"

"Mr. Kelso and I agreed to meet early one morning in the Mount Kisco railroad station. We took the commuter train, as normal as you please. Of course we sat in different seats, as there were friends and neighbors nearby. We were married in the Little Church Around the Corner and that same day we set out on a trip through the New England states. It was early October and the foliage was glorious."

"How often I've heard that story," Irving said in a fond voice.

Alice said, "Actually, this was supposed to be your party, Mildred—you've had us over so often. Giorgio and I weren't planning to announce the other thing until the restaurant—our restaurant—is a going concern. One thing at a time in suburbia, you know."

"Here's looking at you!" Betty said, splashing her wine about in the guise of a toast. "And also to a great boss."

"Of whom it might be said, he has not so much lost a sister as gained a brother-in-law," her employer said.

"No, I am the one who gains," Giorgio said. He was barely prevented from kissing Marshall.

"He is a fine boy—he will make you very happy," Asdrubale said to Marshall with a ribald laugh.

"Anyway, Fabia," Alice said, "you don't have to sulk. You can be pretty 'I Love a Mystery' yourself."

"Who's sulking?" Fabia said, flushing slightly. "Another glass of wine, Memmo, please." The light seemed to dawn in Alice's eyes, and she readdressed herself to her rollatine.

"Now, the cake," Asdrubale said. A thin layer, somewhat sunken toward the center, was placed before Mrs. Grossblatt. "Rice torte, traditional for weddings in the Trentino." Noting the lack of enthusiasm with which it was greeted, he added: "Or you can have the *zuppa inglese*—the English trifle soup."

Alice shook off her lethargy and attacked the torte, as Mrs.

Kelso observed, "That's funny—rice is traditional for weddings in America, too."

"It's more Bennington ware," Victor said, displaying a mottled brown spittoon to his wife's wondering gaze.

"Oh, well," Nadia said, "we can't expect her to unearth an entire President Grant bedroom suite every day."

The young couple spoke to one another in French. Victor's was surprisingly fluent, though he was often complimented on his Swiss accent.

Nadia burrowed further into the excelsior and produced a bundle of old *National Geographics*. "Claire must be kidding," she said, this time in English.

A title on the cover of the topmost number—"Long Island, the Red Man's Paumanok"—caught Victor's eye. He collapsed into a *fauteuil Voltaire* and began to peruse it.

" 'Kansas, the Sunflower State,' " Nadia read from the cover of another issue. "Why do they call it that? I thought sunflowers symbolized Russia."

But Victor's attention had been mesmerized by a cottony photograph in the magazine. "Hey, get this: 'Storied Kelton—once a trading post, now a commuter's paradise.' I know that part—it's near the station," he added wistfully.

Nadia dumped the *Geographics* onto a Duncan Phyfe sewing table and returned to the packing case. Her explorations were rewarded by a long tube, from which she withdrew a lithograph. It was done entirely in shades of blue-mauve, and showed a grotesque child's head surrounded by zinnias equal to it in size. A caption read, "Baby Goliath—Ultimate Triumph of the Hybridist's Art." Beneath this was attached a calendar for the year 1897. "It's in mint condition," she said gleefully.

The jangling of sleigh bells, set off by the opening of the shop door, caused them both to look up. A postman who resembled the young Marcel Proust in military uniform entered, holding a calendar illustrated by what seemed to be a bundle of Virginia creeper. "The new post office calendar," he said.

"How much?" Victor asked.

"As you like it," was the simpering reply.

Victor fished four one-franc pieces out of his pocket and handed them over.

"Oh—I almost forgot—I have a cablegram for a Monsieur Victor Bridgewater. Are you that gentleman?"

In fact, there were two telegrams, one for each. Victor's was from Paul Lambert and commanded them to put another chicken in the pot, against his return to Paris that evening. Nadia read hers over several times before she divulged its text: "ANXIOUS YOU ARRIVE CONSULT IMPENDING DEBUT DISCUSS WHAT HAVE YOU PLANNED." It was signed, Mrs. Wally Wetmore Jones.

"She is mad," Nadia said. "I will not fly all the way to Long Island that I may become immured with mad people."

But Victor had noticed something on the telegram. Fitfully retrieving his *Geographic*, he fumbled through it for a moment and then pointed triumphantly at a certain photograph. When he had recovered his breath, he read the caption to a puzzled Nadia: " 'Plandome—Jewel of the North Shore.' You see, Nads—it's fate—a coincidence," he stammered.

The postman cleared his throat, and Victor responded with a further one-franc piece.

"I almost forgot," the man in blue said. "I also have a special-delivery letter for a Mlle. Tosti, 24 rue de l'Université. Does this lady dwell here?"

Nadia silently accepted the letter and waited for the mock-Proust to leave the shop before she opened it. "Civil servant," she said. "Extortionist is more like it. In fact, I suppose he is some sort of spy." She sliced open the letter and, after a glance, presented Victor with what he was accustomed to think of as a précis. "It's from Mother. I gather that all is forgiven, though she doesn't spell it out. Anyway, we can come visit during the hunting season if you want to."

Victor glanced anxiously at the peeling wall on the other side of the street. "Listen," he said, "I feel we should try to make it to the opening of Giorgio and Alice's restaurant. After all, if we're together, it's a little bit because of them. I mean, if I hadn't been interested in her I might not have become so interested in you."

"What hubby wants, hubby gets," Nadia said, giving him a peck on the cheek. Victor took the hint and finished unpacking the case. Its final treasure turned out to be a banner for a Hibernian marching society, thick with gold thread and heavy with fringe.

A scant two hours later, the Bridgewaters *fils* were excitedly discussing plans over a *poulet basquaise* with an equally euphoric Paul Lambert in their attic apartment. The latter, it developed, had been summoned to Detroit to test a controversial model optimistically destined to overthrow the E-type Jaguar. It was agreed that the three would emplane together for the New World the following Thursday.

"It's funny you were never here before," Irving said, in a suitably lowered voice. "But I guess it's a case of your misfortune being my good luck."

"Had I known," Claire said, "that the terrible Mr. Frick had bought anything like this . . ." She leaned a little further over a velvet rope, the better to study two rouged cherubs in a sleigh. From there her gaze returned to her lapel watch.

"Don't worry," Irving said jovially. "I'm keeping track of the time."

"That's good. I'd hate to miss that Shaker lot at Parke-Bernet. Victor seems to think they'll be in business, as he says, if they can get some. Deal has apparently replaced *Arts-Déco* as the latest *frisson*—craze, rage—in Paris."

"What was that other one—the one Shaker is replacing?" They passed through the atrium, where a fountain played among some caladiums, on their way to the Whistlers.

"*Arts-Déco*," Claire said, " 'nineteen twenty-five style.' Your mother's dining room is a perfect example of it. In fact, if you ever wanted to part with them . . ."

Sadly, Irving shook his head. "Mildred isn't much on parting with things, I'm afraid. She claims it's me she's saving them for."

"Speaking of her dining room reminds me of what a marvelous cook she is. Do you know I made the black bottom pie for some friends in Paris? They liked it although they claimed it was actually derived from an old Burgundian recipe."

They came to rest before Whistler's "La Fille en blanc," as Claire called it. "Weak," she observed, "yet a masterpiece. I'm so glad to have tracked it—that we have tracked it to its lair." She gave Irving a special smile.

"You know," Irving said solemnly, "you could get away with a dress like that. With your hair, I mean." His ears began to redden.

Claire smiled. "Old Sturbridge!" she exclaimed happily.

"What did you say?"

"Oh, nothing. I guess I was just thinking out loud. We must bestir ourselves if we are not to miss the Hoppners." As they continued on their way, she said in a different voice, "I feel so very, very sorry for Alice and Giorgio. What *are* these impediments to their getting a liquor license?"

"Alice claims it's because the mayor's brother-in-law owns a half interest in an English pub down the street. I must say I feel sorry for Marshall."

"Then they each have a little of our sympathy," Claire said. "Let us hope they use it wisely." She stopped and peered through an open door into the circular auditorium, hung with brocade. "I don't suppose, Iriving, that you know the English word for *affreux?*"

"No I don't. But think I get the message. They say *she's* pretty good though." He pointed at a small sign announcing a harpsichord recital by Yella Pessl.

"Perhaps so," Claire concurred. Yet her thoughts seemed elsewhere. "And what of Fabia and her young man? She is the one who gives me real concern. Her parents must suffer a good deal, though they never show it, I suppose."

Irving nodded his agreement. "Mildred thinks so too. She talked to Diana Bridgewater on the phone for nearly an hour the other day, and she says she couldn't get a word out of her."

"I think we've had enough of this." Claire took Irving by the arm. "Let's go sit on a bench by the park," she said, as they sped past a Laurana bust and Blake's illustrations for *The Pilgrim's Progress.* "Or better yet, we can stroll up Madison Avenue. There's a drugstore which has Florida Water in the large bottle."

Great was their surprise on arriving at the celebrated auction galleries to find that not only had the sale already taken place, but that Victor and Nadia had preceded them there. Both Clair and Irving had difficulty recognizing Victor. He was wearing an aubergine-colored suit of extravagant cut, and his hair recalled Mary Pickford at the beginning of her career.

Truth to tell, Claire seemed at first not best pleased, but when Nadia had explained about the cable summoning her early to Long Island, and their other arrangements, she merely said, "Well, if you are confident that Mother's are the hands in which to leave the shop, then I too am content."

"And how is life along the Left Bank?" Irving asked, eyeing Victor with some mistrust.

"*Sensass*," Victor said, then quickly translated, "It's the most."

"Victor," Claire said, as they headed for the bar of the nearby Longchamps, "I can't help asking: has the doctor seen you in that suit?"

"Yup. All he said was 'So that's what they're wearing over there now.' Actually it was Mother who asked me not to wear it to the shopping center."

Meanwhile Nadia was pouting to Irving, "He spends all his time at *le drugstore*. It's all I can do to get him to sweep out the shop."

Irving looked relieved. "I guess he'll always be a Peck's Bad Boy at heart," he assented.

When they were seated round the peanuts and had ordered their drinks—"*Deux Scotch*," Victor had said to the comprehending and indifferent waiter—Claire gave them a brief résumé of what she called her "recent whirlwind and lightning shopping tour." From Cooperstown to Harpers' Ferry, with a brief side trip to Grand Rapids in search of *le borax* which was beginning to find favor in the Faubourg Saint-Germain—her interlocutors were spared nothing. She concluded with a dramatic announcement. After reminding them all once again of her passion for the state of Vermont, she revealed that she had made the down payment on a small house ("*C'est un vrai shambles, tu sais,*" she said in an aside to Nadia) not far from Montpelier. And there she intended to pass her declining years, although, as Irving gallantly reminded her, these were by no means in the offing.

"They may well be over," Claire said, "by the time I have made it habitable. It is on a hill, surrounded by distant mountains—far from any sea, I assure you, though the real-estate agency described it as, 'authentic Cape Cod, eighteen thirty-eight.' After that, it came as no surprise to learn that it is in the township of Calais." She paused. "Pronounced, 'callous.' Ten acres, a trout stream, a maple sugar grove, and no electricity. And the whole area is lousy with antiques. That's where I got you the Bennington." Victor could not repress a grimace. "By the way, how did you do at the auction?"

He rolled his eyes and whistled on two notes. "The prices for that Shaker stuff—they were way out of sight. But we managed to land a mission set: desk, chair and stool—golden oak, bronze fittings, and the original leather's all intact."

"Marvelous," Claire said. "Just the thing for a pair of Roycroft lamps I dug up in Vermont—hand-hammered copper, with those dark green pebble-glass shades."

Irving looked incredulous. "Is Paris really ready for Elbert Hubbard?"

"And how," Claire said. "I've promised myself to make the 'little journey' to East Aurora myself one of these days, if I can ever find the time."

Nadia looked carefully about before she spoke. "The word in Paris is that *Graphis* and *Domus* are each doing an all-Hubbard number. *Domus* gets the houses, and *Graphis* gets all the rest."

"Then East Aurora is definitely a must," Claire said.

"I frequently have dealings with a pencil factory in Hornell, New York," Irving mused. "It isn't far from there. Maybe I could motor us all up some weekend. Mother would probably like to come too. She used to be a devout Chautauquan in her younger days. In fact, there's a rather curious story in that connection." His appearance subtly changed to that of a skald about to smite the harp and give out with "Archibald Douglas." "When Mother was a girl, Elbert Hubbard was the household god. He could do no wrong. Her parents—my grandparents—even paid a visit to East Aurora on their honeymoon, met the great man himself, and spent the afternoon at the surrey races. Well, to make a long story short, I guess you all know that Elbert Hubbard went down with the *Lusitania*.

That night, for no reason whatsoever, Mother sat bolt upright in bed. It's not something she likes to talk about, but I know she thinks about it a good deal."

"Does she believe in extrasensory perception?" Victor asked.

"First," Irving said, "let me ask you a question, which I'll put this way. Do you *not* believe in ESP?"

Victor gave this some thought before he spoke. "No. The way I see it, it's just one of those things science hasn't caught up with yet."

Irving seemed to find this acceptable, but contented himself with saying, "As for Mildred, she has no choice but to believe in it."

"Heavens," Nadia said, "you give me a shiver."

Claire, however, scoffed. "We have no such thing in France —the supernatural is exclusively an Anglo-Saxon preoccupation."

"What about those ghosts at Versailles?" Victor asked.

"You know they waited two hundred years before appearing to some English spinsters, doubtless because they could find no French person gullible enough to believe in them. My house in Vermont was cheap partly because there is supposed to be a ghost in it—that of a virgin who likes to emit hair-raising groans. But I told the agent, 'You do not frighten one nurtured on Descartes and Auguste Comte.' "

Irving looked as though he might speak volumes on this subject if he chose. But all he said was, "I should like very much to see this place someday."

"You are giving Claire," Nadia said lightly, "what I would call a peculiar look."

Irving blurted out what was on his mind. "I just realized what she's thinking about—besides the conversation. It's an article of clothing, something like a sweater or a skirt."

Claire laughed. "It is, in truth, my heather wool suit, which

I have misplaced somewhere in my travels. You impress me not at all; it is just like those messages relayed by a medium: 'It is very beautiful here,' or 'very green.' Besides, when is any woman not thinking about an article of clothing?" she added in her best Gaby Morlay manner.

"Irving," Victor said, "you're scary."

Noticing that Irving seemed restless, Nadia consulted Claire's lapel watch and said, "It is time for the harried commuters to return to Kelton. *La Mère Jones* insists that I report for work at the crack of dawn. She wants the decor to echo the Powers statue, and I must somehow find a million bachelor buttons."

The shadows were lengthening in Madison Avenue when the two couples parted: Victor and Nadia for Penn Station, Irving and Claire for an unknown trysting place—possibly the Rainbow Room.

chapter twelve

"You're going to set yourself on fire," Alice said.

This remark made no impression on Marshall, perhaps because it was lost in the sound of the storm: a polyphonic moaning of the wind and fusillades of snow against the glass. By the light of a guttering candle, he was trying to decipher the directions on a package of frozen collard greens.

"It calls for a quarter of a cup of salted water," he said. "Where did Giorgio put the measuring cup?"

"The last time I saw it, it was in your bathroom." The words seemed not so much spoken by Alice, a dim shape in heavy coat and kerchief at the kitchen table, as by an aged kulak. "If you used bottled shampoo like other people, you wouldn't have to rinse the soap out with vinegar water."

"Please," Marshall said in tones of genuine agitation. "I'm having enough trouble with this meal as it is. Now have we got a two-quart enamel saucepan?"

Alice groaned. "Oh, just throw it in anything. What difference does it make?" Like the sound of the horn in *Ernani*, her words seemed to be the long-postponed but inevitable command. At any rate, the door flew open and the candle went out.

"I'm terribly sorry," Fabia's voice said. "I only meant to knock. Please, won't somebody help me close it?"

Alice rushed to her aid, and after a brief struggle the storm was again shut out.

"Whew!" Fabia said. "I never thought I'd make it. I kept thinking of wolves. Did you ever read Tolstoy's 'The Snow Storm'?"

"Yes," Alice said.

Fabia gasped. "Something over there is giving off sparks," she said.

"It's just Marshall," Alice said bitterly. "Marshall and his heirloom tinderbox. Take off your coat and your galoshes," she added in a more kindly tone. "Marshall, please light that candle. It's not all that difficult."

"Here," Fabia said. She advanced on him, a lighted Ronson in hand. "Have you really only one candle?"

"Yes," Alice said, "and I'm piteously glad to have that. The next step, I suppose, is to float a wick in a saucer of salad oil."

"Say," Fabia said, "why don't you light the burners on the stove? That should give off quite a lot of light. And heat."

Marshall, however, demurred. "And suffocate?" he said.

Even as he spoke the door again burst open and snow blew

into the room, as in an old-time melodrama. This time Giorgio lurched in, an inert figure clasped around his neck.

"Alice!" he called. "Look who I got here! It's Professor Scott—he collapsed in a snowbank. A few more seconds and he'd have been a goner."

Then there was a bustle and to-do. Alice silently produced some plumber's candles from a cache, the living-room sofa was made up as a bed, and Marshall, after vainly jiggling the phone, which had long been dead, set out to fetch Dr. Bridgewater.

Alice wiped away a tear and flung herself against Giorgio's chest. "I feel so guilty for all the mean things I've said about him," she sobbed. "I'd give anything to hear him play the 'Humoreske'—now."

There was a faint stirring on the couch, and all eyes were drawn to it. Professor Scott muttered something of which the distinguishable words were, "My viola . . ."

With mounting horror, the young people realized that yet another rescue mission was in the works.

"It must be ruined by now, don't you suppose?" Fabia wondered.

"I imagine it's in its case," Alice said, adding in an undertone, "alas."

Again the moribund shape on the divan stirred and the others heard the words, "My viola." Giorgio disappeared into the black and in a matter of seconds had returned with the instrument. When the good news was brought to Professor Scott, however, he continued to mutter and, in truth, seemed not to understand. Alice took the viola from the case and ripped off an electrifying cadenza. The professor's eyes flew open and he shot her a piercing look such as Paganini might have given on hearing Evelyn and her Magic Violin. But when Alice had replaced the viola, he closed his eyes and sank visibly into a deep untroubled sleep.

"It wasn't *that* bad," Alice snorted as she stomped off to the kitchen.

"Maybe I should make some hot chocolate," Giorgio said thoughtfully, vanishing in her wake.

After glancing incuriously at the professor, Fabia turned to examine the furnishings of this room she knew so well. The two Staffordshire dogs still stood guard on the mantelpiece, but over it, in place of the Currier & Ives print that formerly hung there, was a reproduction of a Fra Angelico. Impossible to make out the subject by candlelight.

"Part of the Spoils of Florence, no doubt," Fabia murmured, casting her gaze in the direction of the library table, where a pile of well-thumbed *Epoca*'s now divided *The Reader's Digest* from *The American Magazine*. "Plus ça change . . ." and the striking of the Seth Thomas clock echoed and confirmed her thought.

A colorful record album of Verdi's Requiem next caught her eye, and her expression darkened. Could it have been at the thought that Manzoni, for whom the work was composed, was the author of *I Promessi Sposi?* We shall never know, since Fabia remained silent. With a ministering peek at the gently snoring blizzard victim, she quit this suggestive scene for the relative hubbub of the kitchen.

The ambiance had changed. Giorgio was now officiating over various pots and caldrons, while Alice was deftly skinning a large fish. "How is the Sarasate of the suburbs coming along?" she asked, but before Fabia could reply, Alice's face turned ashen and she dropped the fish. "Say—you don't think his fingers got frostbitten, do you?"

"I doubt it," Fabia said. "He had his sealskin mittens on. Still, if you think I ought to go feel them . . ."

There was a lull in the whistling of the wind and the door opened. Marshall and the doctor entered against a background of thickly falling snow through which distant flames could be vaguely seen.

"It's the roller rink," Dr. Bridgewater said. "Where is my patient?"

"We'll be lucky if the whole shopping center doesn't go," Marshall added with grim relish.

Alice and Giorgio stared at each other. The latter, after choking on the words, was finally able to stammer out, "Wha —What about Sir Toby Belch's Pub?"

"I fear it is directly in the path of the flames," Dr. Bridgewater replied. "Well—*au travail*." He hastened into the living room carrying his old-fashioned black grip.

"Marshall, do you realize what this means?" Alice said.

"I think so, but it's a little early to start baking the funeral meats. The Kelton firemen are valiant lads and staunch." Marshall frowned as he looked about the kitchen. "Say, listen, Alice, what about the supper I was fixing?"

"Don't worry," Giorgio said proudly, "it's *here*." He gestured toward a stockpot which was beginning to steam.

Alice appeared overwrought. "Marshall, how *can* you go on thinking about those miserable collard greens at a time like this? It's just like you—fiddling while Rome burns."

"Well, you're not exactly trying to extinguish the blaze," Marshall replied tartly, after lifting the lid of the stockpot and slamming it down again. "Quite the contrary. Besides, what makes you think the pub's demise would have any effect on your application for a liquor license?"

"Why don't you two cool it?" Fabia said.

"She's right," Giorgio said. "Besides, like a saying we have in Italy, it brings bad luck to quarrel in the presence of food."

Dr. Bridgewater appeared framed in the doorway to the living room.

"Alice, I must have a basin of hot water at once," he said.

"Don't tell me it's twins," Alice said. The ensuing laughter, in which the doctor did not join, helped somewhat to relieve the tension.

"I may need your help, Fabia," Dr. Bridgewater pursued. He turned from the door, and his daughter followed without demur.

"That's a departure," said the surprised Alice.

The hideous ululation of a siren arose from the highway outside. The three looked at each other.

"Do you think it's getting closer?" Giorgio asked.

"No, I don't," Marshall said in a kindly voice. "In fact the wind is blowing it in the other direction."

"That's nice," Giorgio said.

Dr. Bridgewater and Fabia returned to the kitchen accompanied by Professor Scott.

"I feel like a new man," he said, "thanks to you, Alice, and your friends. What can I do to repay you?"

This question was left hanging.

"Well, that's over," Dr. Bridgewater said, closing his satchel with a click. "I must be getting back now. Perhaps you should come too, Fabia. Your mother will be worried sick, what with the blizzard and the fire engines and all."

"On the other hand," Fabia said, "perhaps you could re-assure her, and say that I had been recently seen, perfectly hale and hearty."

"Why don't you all stay for dinner," Giorgio said, "and I will go and fetch Mrs. Bridgewater, on my back if need be."

"Now, that's very kind," Dr. Bridgewater said, "but I'll take a rain check—or should I say a snow check—for Mrs. Bridgewater and myself. It's more than a bit too cold for her out—as well as in," he added, as he took in the kitchen, crowded with people all wearing overcoats.

"Giorgio will go with you," Alice said. "Marshall, you can start peeling the potatoes."

"In this light? I'll cut myself," Marshall said.

"Not if you use the peeler," Alice said.

"Can I do something?" Fabia asked.

"Yes, you can clean the fish," Alice said.

Dr. Bridgewater, however, was on to Alice's little ways, and he continued as though no interruption had occurred. "Both in the role of old and trusted friend, as well as that of medical adviser, I must insist that Professor Scott accept your invitation. Make sure that he has at least a cup of that nourishing broth," he said in an aside to Giorgio.

"Will do," the latter replied, with a conspiratorial wink. They bade farewell to the others and once again consigned themselves to the hazards of the storm.

After a glance at the half-cleaned fish, Fabia said, "I'm sure you shouldn't be on your feet, Professor Scott. I'll keep you company in the parlor. I'm dying to hear all about your latest musical prodigies."

"There aren't any," the professor said. "Not since Abel, anyway—and he lacks the faculty of attention."

"If you don't want to clean the fish, you can wash the lettuce leaves," Alice said. "Professor, why don't you sit on that chair over there. You'll be nearer the stove that way."

"I don't want to be a drone," Professor Scott said. "Perhaps I could play something on the viola to distract you while you work."

But Fabia had already manned her battle stations. "Surely you're not going to serve a salad on top of all this. Personally, a cup of broth and a taste of fish would be loads." With that, she guided the professor from the room.

"What was it Lenin said," Alice mused cheerfully, "—those that do not work, shall not eat?"

"How do you want these peeled?" Marshall asked.

"What's that supposed to mean?"

"Last time I was shanghaied into doing this," Marshall said, lackadaisically scraping an aging new potato, "your husband told me to make them look like corks."

"I *was* thinking," Alice said, "of potatoes Anna. But Giorgio says with fish, just boiled and sprinkled with a lot of *prezze-molo*."

"Parsley," Marshall snarled.

Meanwhile, back in the parlor, Professor Scott was reacting to the novel situation of being alone with an attractive member of the opposite sex. His had been a life of austere dedication to his art, although, to tell the truth, he was neither old nor precisely plain. Nor was this lost on Fabia, who had warmed to her work with a capsule critique of the Maggio Fiorentino, of which—to hear her tell it—the high point had proved the introduction for solo violin to the trio in *I Lombardi*.

"Yet it is curious," the professor said after a sidelong glance, "how the resources of the violin have been neglected in Italy since the days of Tartini. The younger generation shows no interest," he went on, lapsing into a formula that came natu-rally to him. "By the way, you didn't happen to catch the Ysaÿe competition in Liège?"

"No," Fabia said, "though not through any fault of Alice's." She treated him to a laugh like a Lalique wind chime which she had picked up at a revival of *Le Postillon de Longjumeau*.

"That's a pity, because some one of the Ysaÿe unaccom-panied sonatas, which many wrongly consider tedious, is gen-erally the final hurdle of the grueling ordeal. Mastering one is, for the budding virtuoso, the equivalent of climbing Mount Everest."

Fabia, at her end of the none-too-lengthy divan, rearranged an old Bush family afghan so that, in Thomas Beer's phrase, it "slushed about her." "Henry," she said, "I've often won-dered—who *was* the greatest virtuoso of the past? One hears this about Paganini, and that about Ysaÿe . . ."

Henry, for such was his name—he had been named after

Henry Hadley, a composer of some repute in his day—had waited all his life to be asked this question, and consequently recited rather than spoke his reply. "To know the answer, at least as regards the pre-Edison period, would be like knowing, in the immortal words of Sir Thomas Browne, 'what song the sirens sang, or what name Achilles assumed when he hid himself among women.' The playing of Joachim, to judge from contemporary accounts, was like the sound of autumn gales sweeping down the Val d'Aosta. In our own time the artistry of Jacques Thibaud is, in my opinion, and despite a certain tendency to mannerism, the closest to perfection. Thibaud," he concluded emphatically, "is a very prince of fiddlers."

Fabia, who had begun to wonder whether a lifeguard was in attendance, decided to strike out for shore. "How marvelous," she said, getting to her feet. "At last I feel I really *know*. But why should we sit here and freeze—surely that's a basket of cannel coal." And before Henry Scott could do the gallant needful, she was deftly tossing the sooty chunks into the grate.

Henry gazed admiringly at her prowess. "Tell me, Miss Bridgewater—Fabia—have you ever seriously undertaken the study of music?"

The ingenious Miss Bridgewater seemed too intent on her creation to give more of an answer than a smile. After a survey of the mantel, she added a generous helping of something called rainbow salts, and topped it off with some purely ornamental cones from a ponderosa, then set all alight with a two-foot match.

"Wonderful," her companion enthused.

As the flames climbed upward, Alice opened the door and called back into the kitchen, "She's found the cannel coal. We may as well bring the martinis in here."

With the change of audience in view, Fabia arranged the afghan in a severely Roman, or "Mother of the Gracchi" style.

"You know," she said, "I'm beginning to worry about Giorgio."

"I'm not," Alice said, as she took in the crackling ornaments. "I'm certainly glad you got rid of those dust-catchers, though Marshall may have a fit."

The person just named entered bearing a tray of tinkling stemware, which he set down on the library table with an irritable crash. "Next you'll be hacking up the Welsh dresser," he said. "Are you aware I brought those all the way from Carmel?"

"I'll send you a box for Christmas," Fabia said. "Fresh ones."

"You can't," Marshall said in the same pettish tone.

"A glance at the back pages of any Sunday *Times Magazine* will prove how wrong you are." Fabia swiveled around on the divan, picked up two martinis and handed one to Henry Scott.

"*Che gelida manina*," the latter said as he accepted it.

A twinkle appeared in Alice's eye as she appraised the situation. "I'll bet you two have been talking music," she said.

Henry flushed. "She shows a keen appreciation of it."

"Fabia keeps pretty busy on all artistic fronts," Marshall said, thus restoring at least his own good humor.

"I wish I could say the same for myself," Henry said, and sighed. "Calliope is a stern taskmistress."

"My, those rainbow salts cast an eerie glow, don't they?" Marshall said.

"Very pretty, no doubt," Henry said, "but I'm afraid it reminds me of an especially trying beginner's exercise—'Up the Rainbow Bridge and Down Again.'" He took a sip of his martini and smacked his lips appreciatively.

"I remember it well," Alice said. "Say, Marshall, I'm getting worried about Giorgio."

"I don't see why," Fabia said. "Mother will have certainly insisted that he come in and have something fortifying."

The rainbow salts, in their passage through the spectrum,

suddenly reached what was, perhaps, the principal ingredient of a magnesium flare. In the baleful light it was noted that the professor's cheeks had become the scene of a rival play of colors. "When I was a student," he reminisced, "at Oberlin, nights like this we would gather round the fire and all join together in a rousing sing. Old favorites, you know, like 'Viva la Musica' or 'Juanita' or 'C'est la Mère Michel qui a perdu son chat.' Perhaps you'd like to try one now, as we await the absent one's return."

"I'm afraid I'm not in voice tonight," Marshall said with a smirk.

"Oh, come on," Alice said. "Nobody's asking you to get up and sing the Haugtussa cycle."

This was all Henry needed. He rushed to the piano bench and burrowed in its depths, then sat upon it. After a preliminary flourish which took him several times up and down the keyboard, he launched into a lusty rendition of "Row, Row, Row Your Boat." His performance, however, remained a solo. By the time the final chord was reached, music had taken its customary toll of Marshall. He awoke with a jerk, slopping a little of his drink on his trousers. At this moment the door burst open and Giorgio staggered into the living room, mesmerizing its four occupants. He was drenched, and his luxuriant wavy hair was plastered to his skull, giving him the look of some Cro-Magnon charmer. The topers by the fire became aware that the blizzard had changed to a torrential downpour. Marshall observed Alice's knitted brow with alarm, and found himself in the unenviable position of one who is trying to change a subject that has not yet been broached.

"Well, well, well, Giorgio," he said, "I see the elements have come to the aid of the Kelton volunteers." Alice's brow cleared and paled, and she emitted a low moan.

But Giorgio's *récit de Théramène* was not about to be truncated. "Yes, the snow has changed to rain," he said, "and I know, Alice, how you hate that. But now hear this—the shopping center, with a few major exceptions, has been spared, but the Sir Toby B. is no more."

Alice subdued her ecstasy with the offhand remark, "If I know them, they were insured up to the eaves—and beyond."

"That," Giorgio said, with a theatrical flourish worthy of Alfieri, if not of Racine, "is not Mrs. Greeley's opinion—and she knows her onions."

Henry, seated at the keyboard, seemed "weary and ill at ease," realizing no doubt that his only course was to listen.

Giorgio drew a deep breath and began. "Hardly had we left Bonnie Brae Avenue behind," he said, "when a *thing*"—he paused dramatically—"like a big puff of wind—hit us right in the face. I had to hold Dr. Bridgewater up to keep him from falling down—he was skidding around on the ice like a chicken with its head cut off. Finally, I got him there—to your house, Fabia." Giorgio paid her feelings the tribute of another pause, then continued *accelerando*. "I pound on the door. Nothing happens. Again, the big puff. I think, 'How can they hear me? In all this yelling wind? It is not possible.' So I lean the doctor up by the door and pound on it with all my force. Mrs. Bridgewater came to the door and opened it. Whew! Was I glad. Well, we got him in the house and loosened his tie, and I gave him a good stiff drink, when suddenly a taxi drives up outside—Victor and Nadia. Victor is wondering what the hell is happening, so we both decide to go over and watch the fire. Of course his mother doesn't want him to go, but he says he's going to go anyway. We start running down Edgcomb, but the police have the shopping center all roped off, but we can see that the movie theater is starting to go. Victor leads me down an alleyway and suddenly we're in Portulaca Road and the flames are shooting up all over. Victor, he sees that the small animal hospital is starting to smolder, so we rush in and try to save the animals, but it turns out it was empty—a lucky thing. So we rush out and two doors away it's the pub that's on fire. Victor yells to the firemen to turn the hose on it—"

"Oh he did, did he," Alice managed to interject.

"I told him not to, but he was like crazy. Anyway the firemen couldn't hear him. Then *we* hear something—I hear something—tell Victor, then he hears it too: like a squeal in the wind. 'Maybe a little puppy dog?' I think. No. Victor saw him first—Abel Greeley trying to get away from the burning movies with a big pile of tin cans, flat ones like antipasto comes in."

Henry, once more the dedicated pedagogue, rose shakily to his feet. "Abel—" was all he could say.

Giorgio reassured him with a traffic-stopping gesture: arm extended, palm turned up and out. "I tell you, that Abel Greeley is one brave kid. He and the projectionist saved the whole Kay Francis cycle—'the cream,' he says, 'of the Huff Society holdings.' Victor and I did a bit too—we got the last reels of *Living on Velvet*. But it's Abel who deserves the credit. Anyway, I'm thinking to myself, if Abel comes, can Mrs. Greeley be far behind? Sure enough, there she is in her squirrel coat"—Fabia made a *moue*—"pleased as punch, with a pile of cans under her arm. 'Well, Giorgio,' she said, 'this may be a sad day for roller skaters and film buffs, but it's one that gourmets will long remember.' 'What do you mean?' I says. 'Well,' she says, 'Sir Toby has just belched his last belch in *this* town. Not one cent of insurance, and they even had an English architect—a pupil of Lutyens, I believe—over here to design the thing and make it look authentic. The Lindblom machine will never be the same again, and frankly I can't say I'm sorry—that nauseating clam dip and those red-faced brokers—brrrh!' And so," he concluded, like an Apollo spacecraft, plunging toward a successful splashdown, "as far as the Trentino is concerned, it looks like it's *avanti!* from here on in."

"That's quite a story, Giorgio," Marshall said. "Kelton has

cause to be proud of her adopted son." Alice looked at her brother in mild amaze, then seemed to find herself more at home when he added, with an eye on the puddle at Giorgio's feet, "But wouldn't you like to get out of those wet things?"

"I'm afraid some details are not clear to me," Henry said. "About the pub and the animal hospital, for instance—I don't quite see the connection."

"There is none," Fabia said.

Henry, taking this for a witticism, said, "I see," and laughed heartily.

Decidedly, the comings and goings of this eventful night had not yet ceased, for a businesslike rap was heard at the kitchen door. Sighing, Marshall went to open it and returned with Victor and Nadia. The former, in ski clothes, was soaked and smudged. Nadia was draped in an old mackintosh of Dr. Bridgewater's and carried what might have been a roast goose done up in oilcloth.

"Hi, Alice," Victor said.

"Mother Bridgewater insisted I bring the rest of their turkey—she feels you must be starving," Nadia said.

"The fish!" Alice exclaimed, bolting past them into the kitchen. She returned in a moment. "I'm afraid it's suitable only for mounting."

"Oh, well, none of us is too crazy about fish anyway," Giorgio said, pouring himself a martini in an old-fashioned glass, a habit he had acquired since his arrival in the United States.

"Me next," Victor said.

"Okey-doke," Giorgio said. He peered into the pitcher, which held only ice cubes and precious few of those, then handed it to his wife. "More," he said, with a certain peasant simplicity.

"I too would not be averse to same—after Victor gets his, of course," Nadia said in a tone of mock reproof. "What a lovely home you have, Alice. Victor has told me so much about it that I feel I already know every nook and cranny. But where is the famous Currier & Ives—'Sugaring Off,' I believe it is called?"

"It's in Marshall's room. Fabia, you show them—" she indicated Nadia and Henry with a wave of the pitcher— "before my husband belts me one." Alice made a fast exit to the kitchen where she was soon heard warbling, "Don't Look at Me Zat Way" in the style of Irene Bordoni.

While Giorgio fetched more cannel coal for the dwindling fire, Marshall distributed flashlights and candles. Fabia then led them on a tour of the upstairs, starting with Marshall's diminutive digs. The room contained little of interest apart from the famous lithograph, which Victor and Nadia eyed greedily.

"Seriously, Marshall," Victor said, "if you ever feel like getting rid of it, I know somebody who collects them."

"So do I," Marshall said. "Actually, I'm not much on the visual arts. Alice just put it in here to get it out of the way. On the other hand, I would never part with it."

After Marshall's bathroom had been inspected, the quintet moved on to the master bedroom, traditionally known as "Alice's room." Victor, in his new Wallace Nutting role, whistled at the sight of the rutilant brass bedstead, while Nadia had eyes only for the green wicker chaise longue. Here, the subdued Italian influence was present only in the form of a della Robbia plaque and a couple of cushions made from Siena palio flags.

In the adjoining bath, Giorgio's presence could be more strongly felt. In fact, when Marshall somewhat hesitantly opened the door, they were almost mowed down by a wave of patchouli and something less than choice of Atkinson's. The eye was drawn to a giant peignoir with stripes of black and lurid red, cutthroat razor and strop, and an open jar of glistening purple pomade.

"Those, I suppose, are Alice's," Fabia murmured to Henry, referring to a pair of nylons and a box of Coty dusting powder.

"I *think* so," Marshall said. "But this place is definitely off limits for me."

The "guest" or "back" room proved a paradise of bizarre and motley objects, at least for the two snappers-up of unconsidered trifles, whose attention was riveted notably by a sinister-hued braided rug and an old Atwater Kent console model.

"The rug," Marshall said firmly, before Victor could speak, "was made by Cousin Bessie—Grandmother Bush's cousin, that is. She dyed every bit herself." He placed the toe of his shoe on a particularly ominous strand. "That used to be part of a knickers suit of mine. It came from McCreery's. However, if it's stuff for your store you're looking for, here's something I'd *pay* you to take away."

He yanked aside a cretonne curtain, revealing in a recess a scale model of Sullivan's masterpiece, the Transportation Building of the Columbian Exposition in Chicago, rendered in a substance closely resembling fingernail parings.

"Oh, Marshall!" Nadia cried. "You *must* let us have it—it's not fair, keeping it hidden away in this—in this lumber room."

"Never," Marshall said. "Cousin Bessie gave the best years of her life to its creation. I couldn't ever figure out why, but Alice says it was the outlet for her two big frustrations: they wouldn't let her go see the Columbian Exposition *or* realize her ambition to be a modern architect."

"What's it made out of?" Victor asked tentatively.

"Toothbrush handles, steamed and sliced."

"I'd like to see some more of your cousin's artifacts," Henry said. "Are there any around?"

"She was no cousin of mine," Marshall said, closing the cretonne curtain. "She was Granny Bush's cousin—that's what

163

we always called our step-grandmother. There might be some odds and ends of junk in the attic, but we can't go up there now."

"Marshall," Fabia said, "you know perfectly well there *is* something else and I don't mean up in the attic either."

At this point Henry, whose flashlight, like his attention, had been wandering, said, "Why, it's 'The Dinkey Bird.' It used to hang over my bed when I was a boy. In fact," he added in a bemused tone, "I guess it still does."

"Maxfield Parrish," Victor murmured to Nadia, for some reason giving the name a French pronunciation.

"I don't know what you mean," Marshall said, "and further-more, I don't like to be accused of prevaricating in my own guest room."

"Well," Fabia said, " 'Daisies Don't Tell,' but I think you may change your mind about the trip to the attic." She guided Henry's flashlight upward, and a drop of water was seen to fall from a dark splotch on the ceiling.

Marshall gave vent to an expletive that made Henry blanch, and rushed to the head of the kitchen stairs. "Giorgio!" he shouted. At once a loud tramping was heard. Giorgio took in the spot on the ceiling and said, "It's OK, Marshall. I think I know what the matter is." A disorderly rout to the attic followed. Giorgio went to the far end and closed and bolted a small round window.

"It was hot like hell up here," he said, "so Alice and I opened the window. I guess we forgot to close it."

"When was this?" Marshall said. "And what in the world were you up here for?"

"Listen, Bluebeard . . ." Fabia began, but broke off with a shriek as a flashlight passed over a dressmaker's dummy clothed in a beaded orange *thé-dansant* frock. "Oh, I thought it was somebody over there," she finished lamely.

"One would think you had never been in an attic before,"

Marshall was starting to say, when a creaking of the stair treads caused the group to fall silent.

"What are you doing up here?" Alice's voice boomed. "I'm getting tired of communing with a turkey carcass."

"Alice," Fabia said, "you've got to get Marshall to tell us about Cousin Bessie's art work. He's holding out on us."

"We'll see," Alice said. "But if you think I'm coming up there to join you in a game of Doctor, or whatever it is you're up to, you're sadly mistaken." As the sound of her steps diminished, that of her voice became sepulchral. "Meantime, the ice melts in the martini pitcher."

Giorgio was explaining to Marshall, "We were just putting Alice's summer things away—there's no cause for alarm, *mon vieux.*" The moist cold had become so pervasive that even the Victor Bridgewaters, after a last look at the attic's murky treasures, joined the retreat to the kitchen. There, a surprise awaited them. The usually scruffy kitchen table had been transformed into a sumptuously inviting buffet, its centerpiece a kind of rose window composed of the sliced light and dark meat of the senior Bridgewaters' leftover turkey, whose garnishes included ribbons and rosettes of pale green mayonnaise. A couple of bottles of Verdicchio were nestling in a plastic garbage can full of ice cubes.

"Alice—you shouldn't have," Nadia cooed. "One would think oneself a thousand miles away—in a *cabinet particulier* at La Pérouse."

"Except for the ice bucket," Marshall said. The spirit of the attic still hung heavy over him.

Just as some were queuing up and others were tactfully asking where to wash their hands, the lights came on. With a smothered cry, Alice dashed at the switch and extinguished them.

" 'Old ways are best ways,' " Henry said to Fabia, apropos

the two silver candlesticks in which stubs of plumber's candles smoked.

"Does light imply heat?" Nadia wondered. The furnace gave an answering grunt.

There was a pause during which many filled their faces. Marshall, waiting for a pretext which did not come, finally enounced, "I suppose you're all waiting to hear about Cousin Bessie. Well, if truth be known, the elephant's-foot umbrella stand in the front hall is a rather unimportant example of her early period."

"That's not what I meant, Marshall, and you know it," Fabia said.

Alice, ever the able trencherman, switched a mouthful of mixed goodies into her cheek long enough to say, "It's not even true," then continued to masticate.

Giorgio took advantage of her momentary inattention to spear a slice of white truffle off her plate. "I cannot tell a lie," he eventually choked. "The Hitchcock chairs—the very ones on which we sit—are a product of Cousin Bessie's fertile stencil. The design, it is said, has some occult signification."

"Oh, pooh," Marshall said, banging his fork on his plate as he stabbed at random oddments. "That's just something you picked up from Alice. About the designs, I mean—they're perfectly traditional."

"Precisely." Alice rose and went swiftly to the Welsh dresser. "OK, Victor," she said, "I guess we owe you a wedding present and this is it."

The young marrieds gaped at what seemed to be a large cube of cordovan leather, with strange grooves and striations. "Cousin Bessie did this one after she was a bit around the bend," Alice explained, none too charitably. "It's a replica of the Carson Pirie Scott Company—exact in every detail. The poor dear never saw it, though. She never got farther west than Binghamton."

"It's priceless," Nadia said, and Victor nodded his assent.

Henry had once again wandered off on his own. "What's in it?" he asked.

"Be that as it may, it's yours," Alice said. Victor had never before seen her in this Good King Wenceslas mood, but he wisely held his tongue.

Giorgio, who had been sunk in a brown study, got to his feet. "You are wrong, Marshall," he said. "The designs—" he pointed to the back of his chair— "are full of occult meaning. Anyone can see it. I can see it. I am right."

"Don't take on so, dear," Alice said. "He only meant that Cousin Bessie didn't make them up—invent them."

Giorgio beamed at his brother-in-law, who said, "Yes, that's what I meant. What's for dessert?"

"Your favorite," Alice said.

Giorgio whisked a pyrex dish containing an amorphous blob out of the refrigerator and onto the butcher block.

"Floating island," Marshall said, in the tone of a judge who says, "Step down, please."

Nadia picked up a candlestick and peered, frowning, into the bowl. "I know nothing of floating island," she said, "but this surely is *boule de neige*—'snaw-balls,'" she carefully enunciated.

"I thought that was baked Alaska," Alice said.

Nadia, who had obviously been waiting for this, gave a little laugh. "No, that we call a Norwegian omelet."

"Though it isn't really an omelet," Victor added avidly.

"Wrong!" Giorgio said triumphantly. "Everybody is wrong." He picked up the bowl and held it under Marshall's chin. "Boodle's orange fool."

"*My* favorite?" Marshall quavered.

"So it would seem," Alice said, "from the way you went at it last week—both at the table and after."

"When are you going back to Paris?" Marshall asked Victor.

"Dunno," was the answer.

"If that's boiled custard," Henry said, "I'll have some."

Fabia suddenly got up from the table and went over to the window. "The rain is over," she announced, "and the moon has risen. The temperature is dropping. By tomorrow that highway will be a glare of ice."

Marshall and Alice warily exchanged glances. For some time they had felt concern for Fabia. Ever since the trip to Europe she had seemed inclined to droop in her cage.

chapter fourteen

The architect of Sir Toby Belch's had lingered on in the Kelton area after the fulfillment of his mission. We hesitate to divulge his name lest it be thought a fabrication. It was Mullion, Godfrey Mullion—a "predestined name." Now that the great fire had taken its toll of some of the town's most imposing edifices, he was the more reluctant to leave a spot which forcefully recalled some of the garden city successes of his post-Royal College days.

One dank evening in February he warily pushed open the great roughhewn door of the Trentino, as it had come to be known, and elbowed his way through the raucous throng toward the bar. "I'm with the Carlsbad party," he addressed the *finta giardiniera* who approached him, eyebrows raised.

"Will you please turn that thing down?" Alice called toward an invisible auditor at the rear of the heavily beamed room.

"I'm with the Carlsbad party," he persisted. "They're expecting me."

"Of course." The manageress shifted the vellum menus cradled in her arm so that all Godfrey could see was: "Valpolicella—$7.00." "Your table is ready," she said, though not to him. "Perhaps *you* would like to wait at the bar."

With a shrug that seemed to indicate his awareness that he rated little better, our Inigo Jones turned toward the bar—and what a bar. The lumpiest glasses Murano ever disavowed were there in a turgid rainbow.

"What's yours, Bub?" a barman who bore a suspicious resemblance to Giorgio Grossblatt demanded. Before Godfrey could answer, however, he was buttonholed by a couple who suggested—in reverse—Chaucer's "January" and "June."

"Godfrey!" Memmo Oscari shouted. He turned to plant an unsolicited kiss on Mildred Kelso's cheek.

Godfrey caught the eye of a barmaid gotten up, he reflected, like one of Garibaldi's Giubbe Rosse. "Your pleasure," she said shrilly.

"A Bombay gibson on the rocks," he acquiesced, then added, inspired, "in a blue tumbler."

Mrs. Kelso beamed at him. "Memmo here has been telling me about the wonderful things you've done at the Kensington Embroidery Museum," she said. "We too are awaiting the Carlsbad couple."

"Is it true," Memmo demanded, "that you knew Sir Sidney Cockerell?"

The architect's drink was placed before him. "Blue," he said, regarding the meteor-like object. "Yes. I knew all of them."

170

"Even Corbu?" Mildred teased.

"I said, 'all of them,'" Godfrey was enunciating through his teeth when Fabia arrived wearing a strapless cocktail-length dress with self stole. "I had no idea, Mildred, that the Italians took St. Valentine's Day so seriously," she said. "Anyway, wasn't he French?"

"Not at all, Fahbia," Godfrey said, "he was a myth." He peered over his shoulder and into her cleavage at the risk of entangling his eyebrows and jacket, cut, apparently, from the same bolt of fuzzy goods.

Noting this, yet still the grand seigneur, Memmo said, "Well, anyway, he was a saint. I don't care if he was a Lithuanian."

Fabia brushed some nonexistent drops from her stole. "Where are those dopey Carlsbads anyway," she scowled. "I'm beginning to believe Victor was right—and that makes me even madder."

"Blast off," Giorgio said. He leaned across the bar and gave her a hearty kiss. "Some dress."

A slight brunette woman in crimson velvet was edging her way toward them. "I'm terribly sorry," she said. "Everett was detained—a last-minute patient."

"For you, Signora Dottoressa," Giorgio roared, "a drink on the house." He grabbed the nearest bottle—Brandy Stock, as it happened—and splashed some into a glass. "After what your husband did for me . . ."

"It was nothing," Leila Carlsbad said, her remark happily lost in the uproar.

Giorgio's already furrowed brow knitted further. "How does it happen," he said, "Memmo, anyway, that you find yourself on this side of the Atlantic? I thought you and Fabia were Splitsville."

"I'll answer that question," Mildred piped up unexpectedly. "Memmo had to leave Fabia in Palermo to help his father diagnose a hitherto unknown form of sciatica. Naturally he rushed back, but was ashamed to say what it was, so he told her it was a final examination, which it was, in a sense. But Fabia knew it wasn't the examination period in the Italian medical schools—so she was reasonably irked. Subsequently she returned to this—well, claustrophobic environment—it *is*, Fabia, whatever you may say—and has been brooding ever since. Then Memmo happened to write me and I told him, 'Come, my lad, come. Faint heart ne'er won fair lady,' I wrote. So he came—on the *Leonardo da Vinci*."

Coincidence, the real Dickensian thing, struck—again, of course. As so often before in the lives of these happy few, the lights went out. In the depths of the dining room a candlelit cake was seen, carried by an anxious girl in a chef's hat. "*Mia sorellina*," Giorgio said proudly. Someone struck up "Happy Birthday"; soon all had joined in; soon it was over. The lights came on.

"Well!" was the consensus.

Mrs. Kelso said to Giorgio, "Your sister is too sweet!" and to Mrs. Carlsbad, "Wasn't she cunning!" Taking her words at face value, or par, Giorgio frowned, and when Mrs. Kelso asked him her name, he barked, "Gemma!" and marched off past the far end of the bar, where some men were pounding one another on the back in what was still good-natured fun.

"Whose birthday *is* it, anyway?" Leila Carlsbad demanded of her husband, who had joined the group.

"Dr. Ernst's," he muttered. "The osteopath. I mean chiropractor."

"Oh that old fraud," Leila said happily. She seemed minded to regale them with an anecdote, but no one was listening.

In another part of the half-timbered forest, Alice was kvetching to Giorgio.

"It's a rum bunch tonight. If there's anything worse than a boisterous businessman, I have yet to see it."

"Don't worry," Giorgio said. "Abel and the Antibodies will drown them out."

"When does he go on?" Alice asked. "He was due here hours ago."

"In fifteen minutes." Giorgio shot her a look full of meaning.

After studying Leila's one-sided smile, Fabia turned to Mildred Kelso. "What's with la Carlsbad this evening? She's as overwrought as an Exbury azalea."

Godfrey gave vent to a heavy and even rabid laugh, which produced a hush. He mumbled. "Azaleas . . . to us English, always suggest 'the rhododendron belt'—suburbia, I guess you call it here." He bent toward his gibson and away from the battery of withering gazes.

Mildred took pity and said, "Of course any cliché can get to be too much of a good thing. Tell me, Mr. Mullion, what's the latest in gardening trends? In England?"

As was his way, Godfrey let the ball slip through his fingers. While he mentally framed an exposé of "heather gardens," a whirling Alice led them to their table, which she "couldn't possibly hold another second." After they had somewhat breathlessly sunk or fallen into their settles, she beamed graciously and said that Gemma would be with them shortly. Long before this happened a cream-of-mushroom voice made them all start. "*Come stai*, Fabia," it said. The group turned to peer at a figure who conjured up Bobby Breen playing the François Villon role in *If I Were King*, complete with measly moustache. It was Abel.

"I got here a little early. *Les copains* had a breakdown, a car breakdown. Man, this place gives me agarophobia. I don't know what Alice and Gigi had in mind, quite. I told them to get someone more like Louis Kahn."

Godfrey choked. His state required some patting on the back, which was forthcoming.

"Easy on the gaspers, old boy," Abel advised. "Don't leave

before we do 'In a Persian Market'—but it won't be till after twelve. That's the earliest Alice lets us plug in the Big Electric."

"I don't see why people can't just have some Italian food in peace and quiet," Fabia pouted.

The others, Abel included, beamed appreciatively, recognizing perhaps that the pout was to Fabia as the bloom to the peach.

Gemma arrived and began dealing menus. "More drinks," she said, "Or you want to eat?"

"Both," Godfrey said.

With the adroitness of a female Harry Thurston, Gemma produced a small plastic-wood salad bowl out of nowhere. In it were nestling olives, radishes, scallions and carrot and celery sticks, around a Druid-like mound of cottage cheese. "Eat, drink, and be merry—but not *too* merry!" she counseled in a soubrette soprano. In a flash she had vanished.

"Godfrey," Memmo said, eyeing some steamy garlic bread with a tourist's disinterested stare, "is it not true that you and G. Herbert Mullion are one and the very same?"

"By no manner of means," Godfrey said, with a guffaw. "I am not quite so old as the Gog Magog Hills, however close my connections to Cambridge and the River Cam. But I follow your line of thought—Godfrey Herbert was my uncle, the one of Omega Workshop fame."

"Ah," Memmo said. He moved the bread further away.

Mrs. Ernst, wife of the birthday boy, rose from that table and moved toward the ladies' room, identifiable thanks to a picture of La Fornarina on the door. "Hi, Leila," she said as she passed.

"Why, hullo there, Leila," Mrs. Carlsbad replied with a smile. When Mrs. Ernst was out of earshot, she explained to Memmo, who was looking puzzled: "We both have the same first name—Leila—quite an uncommon one. We're in the same bridge club."

"In Italy," Memmo said, "it is not uncommon."

Fabia addressed herself to the mural, the latest work from the brush of the artist who had decorated the Golfo Azzuro. It was a breathtaking hemicycle of lush scenery that brought to mind the lines, "From Greenland's icy mountains, to India's coral strand."

"I bet you, Fabia," Memmo said, "Godfrey thinks like I do: how much better if all is painted in pleasant light shades of cream—but very pale, like marscarpone—and maybe just a few hanging lights, style of Charles Rennie Mackintosh."

"Mackintosh!" Godfrey gagged on an olive, but managed to splutter, "that scourge."

"Truthfully, I don't see that as a background for Alice," Fabia said. "Though I know what you mean." She accompanied the last with a private smile.

"Why, good evening," Henry Scott said. He seemed surprised to find anyone he knew at Kelton's most popular water hole. He was, nevertheless, dressed to the "nines."

His arrival affected Fabia like a joy buzzer. "Henry," she ejaculated, "you rascal!" She presented him to the others, making a special point of Memmo in a way that suggested the famous old chromo, "Two Strings to Her Beau."

"Are you traveling here, or studying?" Henry asked him urbanely.

"He hopes to enroll at Columbia Presbyterian in the fall," Fabia replied quickly. "Meanwhile we plan to travel a bit and see some of life in these United States."

The idea of a young unmarried couple doing some traveling together caused Henry's lids to lower. But when Memmo proffered a chair—snatched from a nearby table with a perfunctory *"permesso"*—he perked up enough to sit down and sigh. "I am here," he said, with a shake of his head as he helped himself to some croutons, "on a cheerless errand. One of my most gifted pupils is to play jazz tonight, aided and abetted by another—I might even say, *the* other."

"You can't mean," Fabia exclaimed, all bright young hope, "that Alice is going to cut loose on her cello?"

"Heavens no," Henry said. "She is merely the occasion. In fact, for her to perform would be distinctly preferable."

"Except," Fabia said, "that the crowd here tonight doesn't look all that big on Max Reger." And, indeed, the pandemonium caused by the "post-college" set which had invaded the establishment was fast becoming a Walpurgisnacht.

Godfrey, who seemed always to be wearing an invisible ice bag on his head, contented himself with remarking, "I have always wondered why these suburban communities are called 'dormitories.' "

Henry's eyes bugged. "Have you never read *Eric, or Little by Little?*" he asked. "Or *Tom Brown's Schooldays?* Or—but I'd prefer not to mention *that.*"

Godfrey beetled his brows at him, and such was their tangled growth that there was a distinct illusion of salt wind and screaming gulls. "No," he snapped, "no, I have not. I have, however, read every blessed word Ruskin wrote." And he began to recite a passage, a famous one, from *Sesame and Lilies.* Henry chimed in and they finished in tandem, two new-found chums.

Mildred Kelso took advantage of their bemusement to say to Fabia and Memmo, "If you decide to go out West, I hope you will look in on my sister and her family in Pasadena. You'd like them. They live in one of the original rose-covered cottages—well, that's what they call them but they're more like large bungalows. Pasadena, you know, Memmo, is the rose capital of the universe. It's where they have the annual Rose Bowl Parade—quite a sight, I can assure you."

"I have often heard of this," Memmo assented in tones of utmost gravity.

"Well, you can just bet how much I've written them about the both of you. They can't wait to set eyes on the Sunshine Girl and her Latin charmer," Mildred went on as Fabia winced. "My late husband's brother also has a home in Pacific Palisades, but I don't know whether you'd cotton to him—he's a bit on the dour side, though a good man at heart."

"We don't plan on missing Pacific Palisades, I can tell you," Memmo said. "Dour—what is that?"

"Stern," Fabia said.

"Rocky, hard," Henry put in.

"Unforthcoming," Godfrey offered.

"What sort of in-laws do you imagine I have? He's a sweet old dear but well—the Scotch background—sometimes he's a little near."

"Ah," Memmo said. He produced a rather large address book and passed it to her. "If you would be so good, Mrs. K."

The beldame fished in her pocketbook for an infinitesimal pencil of exquisite craftsmanship, and proceeded to write for some time in a crabbed hand. The others watched as though hypnotized, or perhaps it was merely that no one had anything to say. Memmo gazed at the page in wonderment after she had returned the book. "So many numbers," he mused. "Such a big country."

Glancing over his shoulder, Fabia read aloud, "The Kon-Tiki Apartments, apartment no. 4014, 51138 Bougainvillea Terrace, Pacific Palisades, California 90272."

"As though mapped out by some idiot savant," Godfrey said. Henry looked hurt.

"Say, do you think we'll ever get anything to eat?" Dr. Carlsbad asked. It seemed as though he wished to inject a note of levity into the conversation.

"Perhaps, Fabia," Henry said, "you might be able to use your *bons offices* with Alice to procure us something a little heartier than these staples"—he eyed the raw vegetables and bread, then added roguishly—"or at least a drink. Otherwise I shall be compelled to force Godfrey to play Sir Philip Sidney and give me some of his. For I think I can truly say, 'My need is greater than thine.' "

Godfrey did not appear to relish this sally; at any rate he clenched his tumbler a little tighter. As luck would have it, Gemma happened by at this moment with a tray of assorted goblets, "*complimenti della casa.*" There was no sign of anything to eat.

"Punch," Gemma said. "Punch Trentino." It was the potent new beverage of which she spoke. "You don't never want to eat nothing?" she asked, and stayed not for an answer.

A sip of the punch—a concoction of grappa and various sticky vermouths, ornamented with an unidentified herb ("Edelweiss," Fabia suggested)—drew a prolonged "Mmm," from Mildred.

"What did we ever do to Giorgio to deserve this?" Fabia wailed. "Memmo, I wish you'd go talk to him—in his own language."

"I tell you," Memmo said, "we don't speak at all the same language. He is from the Trentino while I am from the Campagna—"

"And only speak Etruscan," Fabia snapped. Memmo was not about to take this lying down, but fortunately food intervened. "Fit for the gods," as Henry later said, in awed tones. It was a splendidly classic bollito that Gemma wheeled up, complete with green sauce and the bagna-cauda of Turin, which has given many a traveler cause to stay his steps in that austere city. Little was said, though there were many pleased grunts and cries as Giorgio's sister plied a practiced knife; and even

Mildred broke down and took a slice from the calf's head—
"just a bit of the jowl," as Godfrey recommended.

No sooner had the first delectable morsels slid down their
gullets than Mrs. Ernst, having finished a prolonged stint in the
ladies' room, again sauntered past, much as a *merveilleuse* of
the Brummell period might have sashayed along Pomander
Walk, in Bath. "Leila—I've such good news," she gurgled.
"We've persuaded Alice to play a piece on her cello in honor
of Ernest's birthday. Neither of us has ever heard her—she
always refuses to perform in public."

Henry's expression indicated that he did not find the latter
fact all that mysterious.

"What is she going to play?" Leila Carlsbad asked with
some trepidation.

"It's by a German composer—Max Somebody-or-other."

As she spoke the lights dimmed and a hush fell over the
throng. A cone of light illuminated a small wooden chair on a
platform at the rear of the dining room. Presently Alice appeared, carrying her cello and robed in a simple black skirt and
daringly off-the-shoulder white peasant blouse. She sat down,
took up the bow, and waves of melody throbbed through the
smoke-filled room.

"The kid's good," Memmo said, and won a giggle from
Mildred.

Henry's tone, though, was grim, as he confided to Godfrey, "Max indeed. Max Saint-Saëns—the D-minor violin sonata, transcribed for cello *and* minus the piano part."

"Don't judge her harshly!" Fabia burst out in an undertone.
"It's a special treat, for me—"and as the "little phrase" welled
out her hand came to rest on Memmo's. For some moments
they communed in the way of Peter Ibbetson and the
Duchess of Towers.

Wild applause and cries of "Encore!" swept the room as the

piece ended. Alice obliged with a brief potpourri of themes from the "New World" Symphony.

Henry seemed too full for speech; so did Godfrey, though in a more literal sense. When the applause had subsided, rather more quickly this time, a blue filter was placed over the spotlight and Abel and his sinister helpmates began installing their equipment on the stage.

Henry felt it necessary to murmur to Godfrey, "To think that the *Gradus ad Parnassum* should end—*here*."

The latter frowned. "After all, he's got to do his own thing."

"I have no acquaintance," Mildred said, "with music of this sort." She stared fixedly at an amplifying stack from which wires leaked like black spaghetti.

"Actually," Henry said, as he rallied his spirits to the defense of music, any music, "it's an age-old dream: for the lyre, the lute and the dulcimer to speak in thunder tones and yet," he wagged a cautionary finger, "to remain unmultiplied in number."

With appalling suddenness the music—rendered even less endurable by the malfunctioning of an amplifier—broke like a hailstorm over the heads of the spectators. Elsewhere in the cavernous banquet hall it surprised a compact group consisting of Claire, Nadia, Irving and Victor, who were being shown to a table near the stage by Gemma. As they turned to flee, the malfunction became total and the instruments were reduced to the relative whisper of their unamplified tones. This time they succeeded in reaching their goal: a basket of imported bread sticks.

"I thought it would be fun to let Mildred go out on the town without me tagging along for once," Irving said, as he acknowledged his mother's presence with a suave wave. "Maybe later on when things thin out a little we can join them."

"Who is that young man who seems to be her date?" Claire asked.

"That's a long story," Irving said, and proceeded to tell it. When he had finished, he said, "Mildred is just crazy about those kids. She even seems to have forgotten about Fluffy."

Slightly above their heads, Abel and his cello were accompanying some household tympani in a piece which sounded as though a sofa were being lifted and gently dropped. "Do you think that's his *own?*" Victor asked in astonishment.

Irving's upward gaze reflected good humor and bewilderment—two states of mind he seldom found inconsonant. "I guess I'm just a relic from the Borah Minevitch era," he said, "though I have no objection to kids doing as they please—provided no one gets hurt, of course."

Having swept the room with a gaze as purposeful as a finger seeking dust, Claire said, "The decor disappoints. From Alice, I expected something with more profile, more definition—though I don't know why."

Victor shook his head in demur, and Nadia explained, "Oh no, Claire. This time you are wrong. It is just right: it is so 'with it' as to be invisible; one cannot see it until its time is past. More definition would crush some part of the public—make them self-conscious. As it is, all types and ages can come and rub along together. You see they are all having what our friend Giorgio calls, 'one hell of a good time.' "

Irving was mildly puzzled. "I don't see anything wrong with it. I mean, it's what restaurants are like, isn't it?"

"*Saluti a tutti.*" Alice had arrived. "I'm sorry you missed hearing me play the Reger." Her friends look blank. "It was my first and probably last public appearance. I only did it because Dr. Ernst is an old friend—he fixed Marshall's trick knee once."

Though no one seemed quite to know what she was talking

about, this was overlooked in the general feeling of *laissez-aller* which was the note of the evening.

"Where is Marshall?" Nadia inquired. "I would like to see him, and to tease him a little."

"He promised to put in an appearance," Alice said, "if he gets back in time from Duluth."

"Duluth?" Irving wondered. "What in the world would he go there for?"

"You tell me," Alice said sharply. "Or rather don't. I have no wish to penetrate his little mysteries. And *this* is my favorite sister-in-law, Gemma."

The person named swiftly disburdened her tray of its Punch Trentino. "Drink these," she said in her sprightly way. "You forget all about food and keep real skinny."

Unbeknownst to them Giorgio had been tinkering with some wires, and now the Antibodies burst forth in the full fury of their enhanced decibels with another of Abel's compositions, a venomous offering called "Smog." The composer himself delivered the lyrics with just the proper amount of contumely. Food was served, eaten, and the dishes taken away before the final intolerable crescendo came and the blue spot went out. Victor and Nadia were rapt; Claire, indifferent; Irving was balancing pieces of cutlery on the rim of a glass, but with mediocre success. They were shortly joined by Mrs. Greeley, Abel and the three remaining Antibodies, who answered to the names of Ralph, Saul and Ricky.

Nadia voiced her enthusiasm for the work with all the mannered sincerity of her native Passy. "It is a privilege to hear such a work—in such a place. Not since I was taken as a child to the first performance of Boulez' *Le Marteau sans Maître* have I been so stunned."

"Come on, Nads," Abel said, "you're not all that old."

"I keep asking myself, 'What have I wrought?'" Mrs.

Greeley said to Claire, who replied with less than sympathy, "You mean, besides a potential gold mine?"

"Say," Irving said, "who's that beefy guy yelling at Mother?"

The man was, of course, Godfrey. But it was Mildred Kelso who was doing the yelling. She claimed to have found the music exhilarating ("I think it's turned her on," Fabia confided to Memmo) and was in no mood for what she called Godfrey's Colonel Blimpery and snide detractions. "You're just another Churchill," she mystifyingly summed up.

The hour was now far advanced, and the clientele of the bistroquet could be observed drifting out in twos and threes with all deliberate speed. Business at the bar being lighter, Giorgio decided to leave it to the supervision of an aide—none other than the Calabrian Memmo, who had long since fled Uncle Asdrubale's tyrannical yoke for the somewhat different one Giorgio and Alice proposed. It was decreed that the Carlsbad and Bridgewater tables be pushed together in such a manner as to accommodate all the friends at a single festive board, and to allow Mildred Kelso to converse with the hirsute youths who had so unexpectedly opened up new pathways in music appreciation.

Giorgio rested a hand on Victor's shoulder and demanded, "How's business?"

"Can't complain," the novice importer said.

"You know something," Giorgio went on in a lowered voice, "this place: it's a potential bonanza. No, it *is* a bonanza. You know something else? All Alice's doing."

Victor's latent competiveness awoke. "When I say we can't complain, I mean, well, this is our second trip already: we just can't get enough stuff to keep the public—our following, that is—satisfied."

He was far from through, but Giorgio had lost interest. "Good, good," he said, and moved on.

"Did you ever unload the Roycroft stuff?" Irving rollickingly asked Victor.

Sensing his insincerity, Victor made no reply but turned to Mrs. Greeley. She had for some moments been eyeing him and the Tosti girls as though taking notes for a society column. "What is that perfume one of you seems to have on?" she queried. "Is that the 'in' thing in Paris?"

"Heck, no," Victor said, "it's just plain old-fashioned *Toujours Moi*."

"Mother Bridgewater has a large phial of it on her vanity table," Nadia explained, "and kindly let me dab a few drops behind my ears."

Though bested by obscure forces, as usual, Mrs. Greeley was hardly one to quit the barricades after a single skirmish. "Your apartment over there must be ideal," she pursued. "I forget who was telling me how quaint it is. Tucked away under the eaves, on the sixth floor, without so much as an elevator to destory the illusion of life in *Le Grand Siècle*."

Victor laughed agreeably. "It's pretty hard to have any illusions about the seventeenth century in a Directoire garret— even with a view across the river and into the Louvre." He continued in a graver tone. "The building has a pretty fascinating history—Rouget de Lisle is said to have taken refuge on the *rez-de-chaussée* during the *crise* of 1830; it's one of the places, anyway. That's why it appears in a decorated initial "R" of Grandville's."

Mrs. Greeley sank without a trace. When her head finally popped above the surface, she addressed herself to the gentleman on her left, Irving. "And how is our perennial bachelor?" she unwisely demanded.

"Perhaps I can—or should—answer that question," articulated a suave but firm French-accented voice. "Irving and I are to be formally united in a fortnight at the First Methodist Church in Kelton. It seemed only fitting to do it here, where we have so many connections, though we are alas not residents —not yet, anyway. You will be getting your invitation to the wedding—*and* the reception—any day now. You would have gotten them long since had my mother not entrusted them to Esperanza, my devoted but none-too-bright *femme de chambre*, who mailed them fourth class." In her studied way Claire sought to deaden the almost melodramatic effect of this utterance by draining her punch tumbler of its dregs of ice and crunching them in her mouth.

"Did you hear that, everybody? Did everybody hear that?" Mrs. Greeley screamed, then repeated the news, for such it was to most. Abel and his men offered to play at the wedding, an offer which Claire tactfully converted into "some dance music, now," while Alice commanded sparkling Frascati, "on the house."

"What is your reaction, Mrs. Kelso? Had you known?" Ricky asked the lady in question, who had given the impression for some moments of silently keening.

"'I'll thank you to know I did," Mildred said, bridling. "Irving has always come to me first with any problem that was on his mind. People have been saying for years that he's a Mama's boy, and now they'll just have to eat their words. He is, though, of course, in a deeper, truer sense of the word. But let's," she went on, noting the discomfiture of some, including Abel and Irving, "talk about cheerfuller things. Claire tells me she is just crazy about her hideout in Vermont."

"We both are," Irving said, "and so will you be, Mildred. This time of year, of course, it's pretty expensive having the road plowed out and all. But in the fall, when the maples turn . . . ! Up there, they call it the festival of the leaves. That's when I'd like you to see it."

The future grandmother accepted this with equanimity.

Another urgent question had arisen in the mind of Flora Greeley. "Where will you live? Here—or abroad?" She managed to give the word "abroad" a true "ticket-of-leave-man" flavor.

"Here," Claire said, "in Vermont, in Paris, the Limousin— wherever the spirit and necessity take us."

Amid the murmurs and compliments a brusque pummeling of the great oaken front door was heard, producing in the commensals a sensation like that of "The Knocking on the Gate in Macbeth," as evoked by De Quincey. The other Memmo sped to open it and admitted two bedraggled travelers—Marshall and Paul Lambert.

"Sorry—our flight from Chicago was canceled—we had to take a train to South Bend and fly from there," the latter managed to gasp out.

"I hope there's still some cold comfort in the larder," his companion added.

"You hungry?" Memmo da Calabria said. "We fix." And after a quick washup and a couple of steaming plates of zuppa pavese, the two were ready to afflict the others with their travel and/or horror stories.

Mildred Kelso rose with steadiness to her feet. "I want to propose a toast. To my son Irving," she took a sip, or a swig, "and to his bride-to-be!"

"Well I'll be jiggered," Marshall said, and joined in.

"I'd seen it coming for months," Paul said. "Ever since that evening in the Avenue Charles Floquet, where I first met you all—or most of you, anyway," he amended, having caught sight of Abel and his companions and suppressed a shudder.

"Do you have any wine bottles that aren't empty?" Marshall asked Giorgio, in an exaggeratedly peevish tone. "After the tender mercies of the Fred Harvey chain . . ."

"Have some of mine," Leila Carlsbad said, ogling him. "I haven't *touched* it."

"That's the least of my worries," Marshall replied in kind, and quaffed the lukewarm brew.

"Do you all live in Paris?" Saul asked Nadia.

"No," Nadia said.

"Is that supposed to be sphinxlike?"

"No."

"Well, it is."

"I thought all you guys believed in," Victor said, "was music or silence. How about letting the martini generation get in some dancing?"

Saul shrugged and stood up, though in a very bent posture.

"Anything by Procol Harum," Leila Carlsbad squealed. The musicians groaned; the rest were surprised to find the Carlsbads still among them.

"Little pitchers have big ears," Irving said to Flora, who was lost in thought.

"They may be big," Leila said, "but they don't stick out." She shook her head, and one of her scimitar-like dangle earrings passed dangerously close to Irving's cheek.

"They're lovely," Paul said. "French?"

"I should hope so. Isn't everything that's nice?"

"Leila," her husband injected sternly, "we ought to be pushing on. I have an eight-o'clock patient." He leaned across the table toward Victor. "I'll bet you're sorry now you didn't take the store downstairs."

"Why?" Victor asked in amazement.

"Because, now that urban renewal has set in, that block is just about the hottest thing in the area. Butterick Patterns took that space at double the rent you were asked, and they were tickled to get it. That's why."

Victor's and Alice's eyes met in mild irony as in days of old, and Alice said, "I suppose the influx of students to the new manual training school is partly responsible."

"It may have more to do," Godfrey said, "with the fact that I am architectural consultant for this renewal."

"Just what is it you're doing?" Henry asked.

"It's a secret," Godfrey said, allowing the lower parts of his head to vanish into the collar of his jacket.

"Godfrey," Leila said understandingly, "can we give you a lift?"

"No thanks, a walk through Kelton at midnight never fails to inspire me. All that frozen music—or deep-frozen music, perhaps—shrouded in the fogs of eventide—it does something to me."

This remark caused the four musicians to confer anxiously. There were whispers of "Frascati" and "bad scene," among others.

"No, no," Godfrey said. "I mean it. Only a European can appreciate what goes on here"—he paused long enough to hear Fabia murmur, "and he stoppeth one of three"—" 'where children play among the ruins of the language.' " But he seemed uncertain of the quotation and lapsed into silence. Henry seemed to share his discomfiture, but could think of nothing better to do than whistle a tune rather loudly.

As the Antibodies struck up a sullen foxtrot, Flora Greeley turned to Irving and asked, "Are you giving up your job, Mr. Kelso? Your travel plans would seem to imply it."

"No," Irving said frostily. "I am not planning to sponge on my wife."

Claire kindly intervened. "We are not without our plans, but, needless to say, for the present we must keep them under the rose."

"Were you in an auto race in Detroit?" Flora asked Paul, her thoughts moving in an ever-quickening paso doble.

"No," Paul said in some surprise.

"I was given to understand," Flora said, her voice rising to the shrill wheeze of a concertina at some long-forgotten Bal Tabarin, "by several sources that you are a racing-car driver. Have I been misinformed?"

Paul's expression suggested thoughts of, "Who is this madwoman?" "Yes," he said, "yes, I'm afraid you have been. Say, Marshall, tell them about South Bend."

"Why don't you?" Marshall said, "since you seemed to like it so much." Flora led the others in an expectant hush. "Anyway," Marshall went on, oblivious, "I have eyes only for Duluth. That's a place where they really know how to relax and get the most out of life. I could even live there myself. You never saw such steaks."

"What were you doing there, anyway?" Fabia inquired.

"You don't know what Duluth is famous for?" Paul asked incredulously.

"Iron?"

Marshall joined Paul in a chuckle. "No, plastics," he said. "My firm is thinking of opening a branch out there. And guess who may just be heading it. I trust there are no industrial spies at this table," he finished with a minatory scowl at Flora, which produced a particularly rewarding *sprechstimme* giggle. Having brought it to its conclusion, she replied, "Goodness, you seem to think I am some sort of Mata Hari."

"That, too," Marshall said.

"Boy," Irving confided to Claire, "if the way Marshall's blabbing ever leaked out . . . "

"It won't," Claire said.

The musicians held what sounded like a brief dish-throwing contest which proved to be, however, a segue. A loose-jointed beat struck up as the electric strings wailed something like "Barbry Allen." Abel, holding a hand mike, came to the edge of the stage. "And now all you lovely people, an oldie but still a goldy." He began hoarsely to whisper "Begin the Beguine." The souped-up amplification made it sound as though a rushing freight train had been granted speech.

"Shall we?" Godfrey said, as he bowed over Flora. And shortly all were cheek-to-cheeking.

"Was that a joke to tease Mrs. Greeley?" Mildred asked

Marshall as they dipped gracefully past a "pecky pecan" credenza. "You're not really moving to the Middle West, Marshall, I hope?"

"Possibly," the latter replied thoughtfully.

Meanwhile Fabia was saying to Paul, "What *was* there in South Bend, anyway?"

"You won't believe this," Paul said, "but it's true: a Pam-Pam's!"

"Oh," Fabia allowed.

Once again the music bumped through a segue, on the far side of which lay a medley: "Broadway Lullaby," "I'm a Dreamer (Aren't We All?)," and "Treat Me Rough." In the last, Abel managed a creditable imitation of the young Mickey Rooney.

"When do you go back to France?" Leila said to Paul as they Charlestoned.

"Never would be too soon—I mean, I like it here."

"So stay awhile," Leila said. Under her breath she added her own tune to the medley: "Cuddle Up a Little Closer, Lovey Mine."

"I'll see. France is very nice too."

"You're telling me!" Leila almost screamed. "Everett and I were there eight summers ago. The food! I ate so much I couldn't get back into any of my clothes. I soon lost it again, though."

"Milady's coach awaits," Dr. Carlsbad unctuously announced, and Paul took advantage of Leila's distraction to escape into the sinuous farandole.

Most of the other customers had now left. One exception was a stout man in pinstripes who was giving the bartending Memmo a hard time over his check. It was true that the Italian youth's addition was often at fault. And so it emerged when Giorgio intervened. He apologized for "this dumb cluck" and soothed the customer on his way with a shot of ouzo.

The music stopped. Alice appeared beside Abel, arms extended and smiling broadly. "It's been a wonderful gala night," she announced, "and tomorrow's another day. Or rather, tonight is." There was a sprinkling of grudging applause and Abel and his men began softly to play "Three O'Clock in the Morning."

Getting the allusion, Mrs. Kelso addressed her son: "Don't forget that we have a long ride ahead of us, Irving dear. I'm sure Claire is anxious to get back to her hotel and a hot tub."

"A mere bed would suffice," Claire said. "Oh dear. I'm in arrears with my five-year diary."

"Speaking of arrears . . . " Alice jerked her head meaningfully backward toward a framed lithograph. Its left-hand panel showed the pitiful figure of an old man gazing at his emptied coffers in a rat-infested garret, with the legend: "I sold on credit"; while the right wing of the diptych presented an oily merchant eyeing a strongbox which regurgitated banknotes and securities; above was the caption, "I sold in cash."

As the men elbowed each other aside—some of them, anyway—and fumbled for their credit cards, Mildred said in her best "Ihr Glocken von Marling" voice, "Alice dear, Giorgio and I have already worked that out."

"All settled, folks," the *padrone* beamed. "Nothing to pay," Godfrey expressed his thanks in a hysterical laugh, the rest in more conventional demurrers.

Some there were reluctant to end what had passed for a joyful evening. Victor, for instance, said, "I'm so hungry I could eat a wolf. Why don't we go over to the Gay Chico and have some refried beans?"

"I heard that," Alice said.

So it was that the cliff dwellers, after bidding their country cousins good night, moved off toward the parking area, while the latter bent their steps toward the partially rebuilt shopping plaza in the teeth of the freshening foehn.

Printed in Montpelier, Vermont in October, 1975 by
Capital City Press. This edition is limited to 2500 copies
of which 26 are lettered and signed by the authors.